PRAISE FOR THE FIERY TALES

"Evocative, erotic. . . [A] sensual treat!"
— **Sylvia Day**,
#1 *New York Times* bestselling author

"Hot enough to warm the coldest winter night."
— **Publishers Weekly**

"Sophisticated and deeply romantic."
—**Elizabeth Hoyt**,
New York Times bestselling author

"Sure to delight!"
— **Jennifer Ashley**,
New York Times bestselling author

"The most luscious, sexy take on classic fairy tales
I've ever read!"
—**Cheryl Holt**,
New York Times bestselling author

"Sets the classic fairy tale(s) ablaze!"
—**Anna Campbell**,
bestselling, award-winning author

The Princess and the Diamonds

and the

Diamonds

A
Fiery Tale

LILA DIPASQUA

DiPasqua

Copyright © 2017 by Lila DiPasqua
Cover Design: Carrie Divine/Seductive Designs
Photography of couple: © Period Images;
Interior Design by Woven Red Author Services, www.WovenRed.ca

PRINTING HISTORY
First Edition: Lila DiPasqua—February 2017

ISBN: 978-0-9951655-6-4 (trade pbk)
ISBN: 978-0-9951655-7-1 (e-book)

To my two furry, faithful writing companions, Rocky and Holly.

We rescued you.

But you rescued us right back.

CHAPTER ONE

Paris, 1687

"Are you absolutely certain you want to do this, Montfort? You'll be turning on your peers," Renault de Sard asked from behind his desk.

Mathias Paul Thomas de Tesson, Marquis de Montfort, found himself seated in the home of the Lieutenant General of Police of Paris, sequestered in his private study—rather than at his public office.

This was no ordinary meeting. Its secrecy paramount. The mission at hand was to topple some of the highest-ranking nobles of the realm, aristocracy that considered themselves untouchable. Above the law.

Unfazed by the Lieutenant General's comment, Mathias sat back in the silk upholstered chair.

"You need a spy. The King wants his ban on Basset enforced. And I am at your disposal." He'd been eager since Sard approached him two days ago. In fact, this was the first time since Victor's death that he felt any fire at all. "Besides, you know as well as I do they turn on each other every time they sit at a Basset table." He couldn't keep the disdain from his tone. His disgust wasn't simply directed at those breaking the King's new law, but at himself.

He hadn't been any different than those who still gambled at the game. Lord knows he was no stranger to the gaming tables. Women and gambling had been his favorite forms of recreation. He'd enjoyed vice. And with his wealth and skill, the monetary losses had been minimal and without detriment.

Gambling had never really cost him. Until five months ago. Five months ago Basset had cost him the life of his closest friend.

"Yes, well, I have finally impressed upon His Majesty that if we don't make examples of men of high rank, his edict will continue to be ignored—and more prominent families will be brought to their ruin," Sard said.

Mathias didn't need anyone to explain to him the damage Basset caused. The card game wildly popular among those wealthy enough to play with high stakes, Basset could make or break fortunes in minutes. He'd seen both men and women lose staggering sums.

Lose everything.

He'd stopped playing when the King had issued his decree. He only wished Victor had done the same. He'd be alive now. His wife wouldn't be a widow, and his young daughter would still have her father.

Victor would never have lost all that he owned—or committed suicide.

"I quite agree," Mathias said. "Unless you bring to heel those involved who are of the highest rank, the wealthy will continue to pay the King's edict no mind." He stretched out his legs and crossed his arms over his chest. "What do you wish me to do, and how soon may I begin?"

"I like your enthusiasm, Montfort." Sard smiled. "I need you to gather names. Tell me who the regular players are, who the biggest players are. And of course, most importantly, who the dealer is—the one that minds the bank—and reaps the biggest rewards at the game."

Mathias gave the Lieutenant of Police a mirthless smile. "No problem."

"Do you have anyone in particular in mind we can focus on? If we're to make an example of him, he must be highly notable."

Mathias's smile broadened. "I've the perfect man to suggest. The Duc de Navers. Is that notable enough for you, Sard?"

Sard lifted his brows. "A duc?" His brown eyes danced with delight. "Oh, Navers will do just fine. Perfectly, in fact."

It was perfect. In so many ways. Victor lost his wealth to Navers. In his very own mansion in the city—Hôtel de Navers—the Duc was making a fortune from his semiweekly private gaming den. Right under the nose of the Paris police. Without concern. Or regard for the royal edict.

Navers wasn't the only noble who hosted Basset games. But he was the one Mathias wanted to focus on.

"Navers's games are masked," Mathias added. "Only those with funds enough to play are permitted. That includes any wealthy merchants from the bourgeois. The mask allows for anonymity and makes everyone equal while playing Basset, regardless of title. Money is the only thing that is held in esteem at the gaming table. If you lose everything, then and only then are you unmasked. Before you're permitted to leave the table, you are made to sign your ruin."

At that Sard frowned. "How will you know who is who?"

"I've played many years with the same people. It won't be difficult for me to determine who is in attendance. Mannerisms, expressions of speech are not covered by a mask. Neither is one's style of play. No one will go unreported."

"And you've no conflict of conscience or qualms in advising me of each and every person there?" Sard pressed. Clearly the man wanted to be assured of his commitment to the mission.

"None," he said without hesitation. "The rule in Basset is that you have no friends." He didn't have any friends left. At least none like Victor.

For Victor and his family, for others who'd suffered the same fate and for any further such tragedies, Mathias was going to put an end to Basset once and for all.

Nothing and no one was going to stop him.

*****

"Is there anything I can say that will stop you from doing this?" Bernadette asked, worried.

"Or I?" Caroline looked just as concerned.

"No." Gabrielle's response was unequivocal as she studied her attire in the mirror with a critical eye. "I think it looks perfect. The binding around my chest is a tad too tight, though." She squirmed, uncomfortable. "But overall, I think I'll pass for a man."

She was taller than most women. For once, her height was an asset.

Bernadette sighed. "I'll loosen it a bit, but you do have breasts, Gabrielle. You are a woman. For God's sake, you're a princess wearing men's clothing. This mad plan of yours has me worried sick."

"Everything will be fine," Gabrielle said, desperate for the statement to be true. Removing the blue satin justacorps she wore, she handed it to Caroline. She fumbled with the closures on her breeches a bit before opening them and pulling out the shirttails.

Her plan had her more than a little anxious, too, but she refused to show her unease to her two closest confidantes, her ladies-in-waiting. Both distant cousins, they were a few years older than Gabrielle and the only ones she trusted to take with her on this secret trip from Versailles to Paris.

The only ones she'd divulged her true intentions to. There were only three people she trusted in the world, her half brother Daniel and the two women before her.

"Hold up your arms," Bernadette said, slipping her hands under the shirt and loosening the binding around Gabrielle's breasts. "There, is that better?"

Gabrielle took a deep breath. "Much better. Thank you." She readjusted her clothing and accepted the justacorps Caroline handed to her.

"What if the King realizes you're not in the country with your uncle at his château?" Bernadette asked.

"Never mind that." Caroline waved off Bernadette's comment. "What if His Majesty learns you stole some of the royal diamonds and intend to gamble them at the *Basset* table? He's put a ban on the game." She shook her blond head. "I don't even want to think about what he would do!"

"The King has done nothing to enforce the ban. And as for the diamonds, I didn't steal them. I'm borrowing them. Stealing implies I intend to keep them. I don't," Gabrielle said. "They'll be returned once I win enough to cover Daniel's debt." Listening to Caroline carry on only spiked her fears. She knew what she was doing was risky, but really, what choice did she have? "I'll not abandon him. He is barely seventeen and they took advantage of him."

Her half brother was not in the habit of gambling. He was coaxed and bamboozled into it by those much savvier than he, and it infuriated her.

"At seventeen, he is a man, has been a man for two years now. He should have known better than to gamble and lose a vast fortune—at an *illegal* game," Caroline argued.

"There are those twice his age and older who have been lured to the Basset tables," Gabrielle countered. She adored Daniel and was crushed when their mother, who had once been the King's mistress, passed away. She'd lost her mother and Daniel in the same week. He was removed from the palace—sent to live with his father's family. The King having legitimized all his illegitimate children from his many mistresses had lost interest in her mother once Gabrielle was born. She'd married the Baron de Leclerc, Daniel's father, shortly thereafter, but sadly he'd died within the first year of their marriage.

The King had permitted Daniel and her mother to remain at the palace, close to Gabrielle, but once her mother was gone, her beloved brother was torn from her. He was only eight.

They'd been inseparable until then.

She wrote to him constantly. Worried about him always. Missed him madly, for she rarely saw him.

When he came to her last week and told her what had happened at the Duc de Navers's hôtel, Gabrielle was devastated for him.

He was in financial ruin. He couldn't pay his servants. Couldn't maintain his château.

She refused to see him financially destroyed. It was difficult enough seeing him so heartbroken and dispirited. Daniel would do anything for her. No matter what. She, in turn, would do anything for him. Including taking some of the Crown gems and using them to win back Daniel's fortune.

"I'll not see my brother destitute, Caroline." Gabrielle picked up the periwig off the bed and placed it over her hair. If she didn't help him, no one else would. No one in his father's family or on her mother's side would ever cover his gambling debt. Especially one so sizable.

And the King had never cared a whit about Daniel.

Bernadette swiped an errant curl from her cheek, her dark hair a sharp contrast to Caroline's fair coloring. "We don't wish to see him destitute either. We're just . . . well, we're most concerned about your scheme."

"I know you are." Gabrielle placed her hand on Bernadette's shoulder. "But I am no novice at Basset. I've played many times at court with His Majesty and the courtiers—until the King banned the game. I'll do fine." She was far better than most. "I'm not without wit and luck," Gabrielle added.

One didn't survive the politics and intrigue at court without having a good dose of both.

Or without being resourceful and clever.

Gabrielle had fooled His Majesty into believing she was visiting with her uncle. Fooled her uncle into allowing her the use of his private townhouse in the city while he was in the country at his château. With no funds at her disposal—for members of the royal family didn't carry coin—she'd thought of a solution and slipped away from the palace with a pouch of diamonds. She'd even managed to turn her entourage of musketeers back to the palace without raising suspicion.

Trickery and deception weren't things she liked. But they were part of her world and deeply entrenched in the royal palace.

Being a convincing liar was more than an essential skill at court.

Her skills in dupery were finely honed after her mother's death. Only then, when she found herself alone in the palace without her mother's protection, did she learn just how much her mother had shielded her from. Duplicity hadn't come easy to her at first. Her conscience had weighed on her in the beginning.

Now she was numb to it.

Besides, desperate situations required desperate measures.

She had two weeks.

Clearly, luck was on her side; she'd made it to her uncle's townhouse in Paris. From here she had easy access to the Duc de Navers's gaming den at his hôtel—and what amounted to four nights of Basset.

If she was to succeed in recouping Daniel's losses and not lose the diamonds she'd gamble with, luck had to remain on her side.

She couldn't—wouldn't—fail. Nothing would get in her way.

CHAPTER TWO

"Ten wins. Seven loses," the banker said, placing four gold louis in front of Mathias. He was up four hundred *louis d'or* already.

It was night and a large solid silver torchère in each corner of the Duc de Navers's drawing room illuminated the three Basset tables.

And the masked players.

Mathias cast the occasional furtive glance about the room. One by one, he carefully studied each person, certain he knew the identity of at least seven in the small crowd. Including the banker at his table and the banker's assistant—the *croupière*.

The banker had all the advantage in Basset, and tonight the banker was the Duc de Navers's own nephew, the Marquis de Raigecourt. He'd know him anywhere. The tall boney man's distinct features were easily recognizable, despite the black demi-mask he wore. Navers himself was by his side—sans a mask—acting as the game's *croupière*. At times there were many cards in play. It was the *croupière's* responsibility to supervise, watching the cards so that nothing that was in the banker's favor would be missed.

Despite his winnings, despite his success in identifying a number of men in the room, Mathias felt edgy. His stomach was as tight as a fist. A barrage of emotions gored his gut.

This was more difficult than he'd imagined. Being here playing Basset inspired thoughts of Victor.

He hated being in a gambling den again.

Hated it that he hadn't tried harder to convince Victor to stop playing when he saw his losses getting out of hand.

And he hated it that at one of the other tables was one of the Lieutenant General's sergeants. Valette, Sard had called him. He was to be his assistant on this mission. He didn't need an assistant and he didn't see how the somber sergeant added to or aided in the task at hand.

Mathias turned over three cards and placed a bet—ten *louis d'or* stacked on each. *Jésus-Christ*, he wanted to leave. *You're helping to put an end to this game that has brought many to ruin. It's the least you can do for Victor.* It was the only thing keeping him from walking out of the stifling situation.

Vaguely he heard the door open behind him, then a brief exchange of words between the doorman and another patron before a slender young man approached and sat down at his table, now making the players total six.

A young man Mathias didn't recognize.

The doorman approached and whispered in Navers's ear. Navers halted play and turned his attention to the newly arrived player.

"My doorman tells me you don't have any *louis d'or* to bet with," Navers said.

"That's correct. I don't," the young man admitted, the pitch of his voice slightly odd. Almost forced. His interest piqued, Mathias studied him closer.

There was something almost . . . captivating about him.

Below the youth's brown demi-mask, there was a delicate jaw. And lips that were, well . . . *pretty*.

"No currency other than *louis d'or* is acceptable." Navers's annoyance laced his tone. "No Spanish *pistoles* are allowed."

"That's excellent, because I don't have any Spanish *pistoles* either." The young man smirked. *A cocky youth.*

Navers laughed, completely without mirth. "Then what the bloody hell do you intend to bet with?"

The youth pulled out a velvet pouch from the breast pocket inside his brown justacorps, loosened the silk ties, and spilled its contents onto the table. A number of pea-sized diamonds tumbled out and twinkled back at them.

Astounding everyone at the table. Including Mathias.

"Basset is a game of high stakes. That is part of the thrill," the youth said. "It isn't uncommon for people to play for lands . . . and jewelry. This one right here"—he flicked one of the diamonds—"is worth five hundred *louis d'or*. I'll start my bidding with it." He scooped up the other diamonds and placed them back in the pouch.

The Duc, like a dog about to be given a bone, was practically salivating. A large grin formed on his round face. "Welcome to the game."

Mathias, on the other hand, was far more gripped by the sight of the youth's hands. Delicate slender fingers. Too refined to be male. Scrutinizing the new arrival closer, he noted the justacorps he wore was of quality and yet was ill-fitting. Too loose in the shoulders. Anyone who could afford a costly overcoat like that would have had the thing properly tailored.

And then there was the youth's cravat. He wore it oddly higher than was the norm, covering most of his throat, keeping Mathias from seeing the distinct masculine feature of an Adam's apple.

He couldn't shake the feeling that the concealment was done intentionally.

Much of the young man's face was hidden behind the mask and the periwig. Since they weren't at court, no man in the room—save for the Baron de Ragon at the other table—wore the itchy thing, and the Baron only did so because he was concealing his baldness—just like the King. It was the very reason His Majesty had made it mandatory for all gentlemen of quality to sport the periwig at court.

Mathias himself detested them. He detested being at court and all its pomp and circumstance and had only attended twice—briefly.

It wasn't common to see a periwig on someone this young—outside the palace.

Mathias's suspicions continued to mount as his gaze dropped to the youth's chest. His justacorps was open and beneath was the usual long vest one expected to find, but it was in shadow thanks to the chair he happened to occupy and the positioning of the nearest torchère. There was no way Mathias could see clearly if there was a hint of female breasts there.

Yet as he moved his focus back to the youth's mouth, mentally tracing the lush curve of his lips, the slender neck, the delicate movements of the hands, his every instinct told him this was no male youth.

He knew a woman when he saw one. He'd spent too many years indulging in debauchery not to be certain.

Why was she concealing her gender? Women were permitted to play. Perhaps she was afraid that if she lost and needed someone to cover her losings, she'd be beholden to the man who advanced her funds in ways she didn't wish to be.

He'd known a few ladies of quality who'd paid off their debts with sexual favors—though none would ever admit to it. Perhaps this was the very thing this woman wanted to avoid. Numerous questions whirled through his mind.

Who was she? Didn't she have a husband or any male in her life who could have stopped her from donning her outrageous attire, traveling through Paris at night to an illegal gaming den to gamble at an illegal game?

If Mathias wasn't taken aback enough by her disguise and actions, he was completely leveled by the sheer daring of her play. She played with confidence. The very same confidence exuded from her speech and mannerisms.

Luck was with her, perched firmly on her shoulder, in fact. She obviously knew it. It made her dauntless. In his opinion, a tad reckless.

And yet he watched her win her *couch* and then proceed to make a *paroli,* clearly after a *sept-et-le-va*—a chance at winning seven times her sizable bet. But only if her winning card was dealt yet again by the banker.

And it was.

In stunned amazement, he watched her indicate she was going for a *quinze-et-le-va*—fifteen times her bet on that same card. The odds of it turning up again, slim. And yet, to the Duc's horror and the awe of every player at the table, her card turned up a third time.

He'd never seen such adventurous play rewarded so favorably so quickly. She'd only just started and had already won a sizable sum.

Then she did the most amazing thing of all. She gathered her diamonds, having not lost a single one, and her stacks of *louis d'or,* dropped them into a pouch and into her pocket. And quit the game.

When that amount of good fortune was on your side, he didn't know anyone who could have resisted the lure to play on for more winnings. Yet she'd stopped when she was ahead—well ahead.

Before her luck could run out.

He was more than a little intrigued by this intriguing woman.

The moment she rose, Navers was on his feet. "You're not leaving already, are you?"

"Yes."

"Why don't you sit back down. I'll see that some of my finest brandy is brought out and some food—for everyone. The night is young. Come now, have a seat. Let's play another round or two while the servants attend to your needs." The Duc, like everyone else, knew the longer she stayed, the more likely it was that her luck would change, and the Duc could recoup the losses he'd suffered because of her.

"No. I'm interested in neither your brandy nor the food. I am, however, tired of playing." The way she spoke, with a certain elevated importance, told him she was of significant rank. A member of the house of Bourbon, maybe? Perhaps she was a part of the Prince of Condé's family? *Merde.* That was absurd. To think that she'd be related to the King's own cousin was ludicrous—as ludicrous as believing she was one of His Majesty's own issue.

As if a royal princesses could or would slip away for this or any other nocturnal escapade.

What on earth was this woman about?

She moved around the table but the Duc stepped in front of her. "Will you be here Saturday night?"

At that she smiled, the most adorable dimple appearing near the corner of her mouth.

Mathias was suddenly gripped by an incredible urge to rip off her mask and wig for a better look at her appealing features. He couldn't pinpoint her age. Try as he might, he couldn't picture her face.

"You'll have me and my diamonds back?" she said in that odd voice she was using.

"Of course. Until Saturday, then." Navers personally escorted the mysterious woman to the door, giving no indication he'd noted her true gender.

Riveted by the way the woman had played, Mathias's concentration on his own game had gone awry. He'd lost half his winnings, and he used it as an excuse to leave. "My luck has turned on me," he said, rising, slipping his coin into his pouch and tucking it into his inner breast pocket. "I'm taking a break."

Valette, still playing at the other table, gave him a curious look.

Mathias responded with a look of his own. One that said, *stay put.*

He moved around the tables slowly, trying not to make it obvious that he was following the "youth" who had just left, forcing himself to keep to a stroll and not bolt from the room after her.

But once outside the drawing room, Mathias picked up his pace, his long legs eating the distance to the doors that would lead to the courtyard—where he'd likely find her and her carriage.

He pushed open the doors and stepped outside, a warm summer breeze wafting up to greet him. There were a number of carriages lined up in front of him. The sounds of crickets and nickering horses drifted though the night air. Glancing in both directions, he spotted her ahead in the distance and raced to her as she made her way steadily and swiftly up the cobblestone path.

"You there!" he called out, arresting her steps.

She turned, her mask still on her face, yet he could tell she wasn't pleased he'd stopped her.

Mathias walked up. It was the first time he noted just how tall she was. Normally with his height, he towered over women. She reached above his shoulder. *The perfect height for a taste of that lush mouth* . . . Having no idea where that errant thought came from, he shoved it aside.

"That was quite the game you played," he said.

"Thank you. I wish I could say the same about you." She turned and walked away, dismissing him completely.

Mathias choked on a mirthless laugh, stunned. *Dieu.* She'd just dealt him a sharp snub. Not something he was used to receiving—especially from a woman. Then again, she wasn't a typical female. He didn't know any woman who would don a man's attire. Or played Basset the way she did.

Watching her walk away, he glanced down her body, noting her long luscious legs clearly visible in her male clothing. He loved shapely legs. She definitely had those.

"I can't imagine why you need to dress like a man to play," he called out. That stopped her steps.

Gabrielle was fixed to the spot. She heard him approach. Her heart pounding so hard, she feared he could hear it.

The man standing behind her was the very reason she'd stopped playing. The weight of his regard had been on her the entire time she was at the Basset table. He had the most piercing light-colored eyes she'd ever seen. She felt as though his clever eyes could read every thought in her head. Know her every secret.

Unsettled, she walked away, fearing she'd lose her concentration, then her luck, the longer she sat across from him.

Undeniably, he was observant. No one else at Navers's hôtel had noticed she was a woman.

Get away from him. Fast. He was trouble. There weren't many people who could rattle her.

Yet, he had.

She turned and faced him, forcing herself to look him in the eye. "Sir, I have some advice for you. If you wish to play better, you might consider avoiding intoxication. It muddles the mind. Clearly, drink has you thinking quite absurdly." Thankfully her tone didn't belie her inner distress.

Amusement flashed in his eyes and he shook his head. "*Dieu*, you are a spirited little piece, aren't you?"

"What I am is bored of this conversation." Did she sound convincing?

The meddling man didn't seem as put off by her impertinence as she'd hoped. Still smiling, he pulled off his mask and ran his fingers through his hair.

Her agitated heart gave a lurch.

Gracious God . . .

Against her will, she drank in his handsome face, his cheekbones, his masculine jaw, and his alluring mouth. Even with his mask on, she could tell, seated across from him at the Basset table, that he was attractive, but without it, he took her breath away. She could better see his eyes now, and they were a stunning contrast with his dark hair. The night's silver light was too dim to allow her to determine their true color, but his eyes were seductive. Disarming. Dangerous. Especially since his mere gaze on her was warming her blood and fluttering her insides.

His male beauty unbalanced her, and she couldn't imagine why.

There were plenty of handsome men at His Majesty's palace, but this man stood head and shoulders above them all—in more ways than one. He was so deliciously tall. She'd always hated her height. It wasn't an asset for any woman to be at eyelevel with a man. Or taller in some cases. But standing near this man, she actually felt small and feminine. A first.

Leave now, her instincts screamed. "Good night and good luck." Her response was purposely curt and dismissive. She turned toward her carriage, but he caught her arm, surprising her and halting her progress.

Her head snapped toward him. "Unhand me!" she demanded, unnerved by the thrill that shot up her arm from his touch.

"Are you always this rude?" he asked.

"Oddly, I had the same question for you," she countered and yanked her arm free, as furious as she was flustered. "Is it your habit to follow strangers and make nonsensical accusations?"

The corner of his mouth lifted into what amounted to a smirk. Then he stunned her by stroking the back of his fingers along her jaw and down her cravat-covered throat.

She jumped back, his caress sending tiny tingles lancing into her womb.

"You are no man, or boy," he said. "I know a woman when I see one, and when I feel one. This game you are playing isn't without consequences. You've won yourself a sizable sum. Do not return here on Saturday. You don't want to become mixed up with this."

Oh, this man needed to be put in his place, so that he didn't become a problem. Her situation was complicated enough.

She didn't need more problems.

"I have the Duc's personal invitation to attend. And I shall attend on Saturday," she stated unequivocally. "You're the one who should stay away, since I'm sure you don't want to part with more of your *louis d'or*."

She turned yet once again, intent on marching away, when she felt her mask and periwig yanked off her head.

She squeaked in surprise, and spun around. Standing there, holding her mask in one hand and the periwig in the other, he had an expression of utter astonishment.

"*Jésus-Christ* . . . You're *beautiful*," she heard him whisper. "Who the bloody hell are you?" he asked forcefully.

Panic surged up inside her. Gabrielle bolted for her carriage. Her pulse racing. Not waiting for her footman, she yanked the door open herself and practically threw herself inside. "Go!" she shouted to her driver, slamming the door shut.

The carriage lurched forward, knocking her from the edge of her seat, where she'd just settled herself, onto the carriage floor with jarring force. Pain shot up her arms and thighs. She barely caught her cry.

Picking herself off the floor, Gabrielle settled back in her seat, her breaths sharp and shallow. An alarming thought ripped through her mind, and she grabbed her breast pockets. The moment she felt both pouches, the one with the diamonds and the other with her winnings, relief flooded through her.

Already she'd won back half her brother's debt. Another night like tonight and she'd have all she needed. But now there was an obstacle in her path. A tall dark stranger. One who inspired dread and unwanted feminine reactions. She simply had to return on Saturday.

There was no doubt in her mind; *he'd* be there.

What was she going to do?

There are only three days until Saturday. You'd better think of something, Gabrielle.

*****

Mathias craned his neck, watching the townhouses thread by from inside his moving carriage. He'd raced to his driver, shouting out orders to follow the mysterious woman's carriage at a discreet distance. Without a second thought. A completely uncharacteristic impulsive act for him.

Merde. More questions were whirling in his head. He was no untried youth. He'd seen a pretty face before, but when the moonlight illuminated hers, a bolt of lust rocked him so hard, it shifted the ground beneath his feet. She was nothing short of ravishing. He'd never seen a lovelier face. He'd never seen her at all. Anywhere.

And he'd never had such a stunning physical reaction to any woman, especially one who hadn't so much as touched him. He was still fucking hard.

Mathias shifted in his seat, trying to alleviate his discomfort.

Though undoubtedly a full-grown woman, she was younger than he'd imagined by her comportment.

His carriage slowed down, then finally stopped. His footman opened the door to the carriage. Dropping the mysterious woman's items he was still clutching in his hands onto the seat, Mathias stepped down. He recognized this street. Exclusive stately townhouses for the social elite.

If not for the full moon, he wouldn't have been able to make out much.

"There, my lord, the fourth one in." The footman pointed up the street. "That is the one the carriage turned into."

Mathias silently studied the townhouse from a distance. It had a rosy-white façade, just like the others near it. By tomorrow he'd know who owned the fourth townhouse.

He wasn't going to wait until Saturday to talk to her. She was determined to return to the Duc's gaming den. He'd seen it in her eyes.

Mathias wanted to know why.

Face it, you want to know who the hell she is. You want to know everything about her—including just how good she'd taste. She'd left him utterly seduced, with a pulsing prick, and the powerful urge to melt that icy façade. There was fire behind those big beautiful dark eyes. He'd seen an instant spark of desire in them when he'd caressed her. Though her tongue could be sharp, he knew down to his marrow that he could coax her to put it to better use.

He didn't want to see her become entangled in the impending trouble about to befall those frequenting Navers's Basset tables. He couldn't speak of his mission, but he could make sure she was steered away. And if she was looking for nocturnal amusements, he'd be happy to provide a new form of entertainment—one of a carnal nature—for her.

Dieu. He rubbed the back of his neck. He couldn't remember the last time he'd been this captivated by a female. For the first time in the five months since Victor's death, he felt the gloom that had descended on him lift. And he couldn't be more grateful.

By tomorrow night he'd know the identity of the woman he had to thank for the small reprieve.

He'd know all the answers to his multitude of questions. Not only was he sure of it, he was looking forward to it.

The next time they'd meet, he wasn't about to let her run away.

CHAPTER THREE

"I still cannot believe how much gold coin you won!" Bernadette exclaimed, closing her book and resting it on her lap.

It was the third time in the last hour she'd repeated that same statement. Bringing the total to twenty times today.

Offering Bernadette a polite smile, Gabrielle closed her own volume, settled back in her chair, and relaxed her shoulders. She hadn't realized she'd been sitting practically on the edge of her seat, her muscles tense.

She couldn't relax. She couldn't concentrate on the book of poetry. It wasn't simply because of Bernadette's or even Caroline's constant interruptions and carryings on about her winnings last eve.

It was because of the confrontation with a man outside her carriage whose physical appeal was far too potent for her liking. One who was meddling in her affairs.

Last eve, she'd shoved the pouch of diamonds under her mattress and had tossed and turned all night, worried about just how much of a problem he was going to be, about what would happen to Daniel if she didn't succeed in winning back the money he'd lost.

About losing the diamonds in the game if her luck turned on her.

Now, it was almost suppertime, and she was exhausted.

Caroline closed her book as well. Setting it on her lap, she rested her hands on it. "Are you quite certain you still have all twenty diamonds?"

"Yes, don't worry. I counted them before putting them in a safe place." Gabrielle tried to sound reassuring despite the numerous doubts assailing her. But she kept her doubts to herself. Though Caroline and Bernadette were her closest companions, there was much she didn't share with them. In truth, there wasn't anyone she completely confided in.

After she lost her mother and Daniel, her heart broke. Left at the palace with no one to protect her, no one to trust until Caroline and Bernadette came along, she learned to cope by holding her tongue, distancing herself from everything. Detaching from everyone at court.

The backstabbing and jostling between her half sisters, between the courtiers—all for the sake of gaining the King's favor—no longer affected her. She'd taught herself not to react to it. Not to trust easily.

In a world where she had little control over her destiny, she could at the very least control how things impacted her.

No one at court could hurt her—because she simply didn't care. And there had been many who had tried to hurt her in the eyes of the King.

She, unlike her half sisters, didn't vie for her father's attention. She didn't waste a moment's thought about whom the King would select as her husband.

He wouldn't matter to her either.

Only Daniel, Bernadette and Caroline mattered, and even they were kept at a certain arm's length.

"You know, at first I was quite agitated over your plan," Bernadette said. "But now, I must say, I do believe you are going to succeed." She smiled.

Gabrielle maintained hers, hoping it looked genuine. "Thank you, Bernadette."

"And you didn't encounter any real problems?" Caroline asked.

How she wished Caroline would leave the matter alone. The questions about last night added to her fatigue. "I've already mentioned, Caroline, that I encountered a small problem. But it was nothing I couldn't handle."

"Yes, but you won't say how small or what the problem was," Caroline pressed.

"It was small. Nothing for you to worry about. Now then, let's return to our reading, shall we?" As she opened the volume to where she'd left off, hoping to lose herself in its prose, she stared blankly at the page, her anxieties about the Basset game on Saturday welling up inside her again.

She simply had to attend. There was no choice in the matter.

Just then, an argument drifted up the hallway and into the study snatching Gabrielle from her thoughts. Glancing up from her book, she noted the dismayed expressions on her companions' faces as the voice of the majordomo eclipsed another male voice. Gabrielle rose and dropped her book on her chair, intent on investigating the disturbance, when the meddlesome man from last night strode—bold as could be—into the room.

Her stomach dropped.

She couldn't believe he was here. She couldn't believe how good he looked. She didn't think it was possible, but he looked even better than he did last eve. In the bright light of her uncle's study, with its many wall sconces and candelabras aglow, his striking male features were illuminated.

And devastating to behold.

His magnificent height, his broad shoulders, his . . . Oh God . . . *gray* eyes, no, they were more than gray. They were a stunning light silver color that set her insides aquiver.

He stopped dead in his tracks the moment he made eye contact with her.

"Monsieur!" The majordomo came running into the room. "My orders are that no guests are permitted—"

Gabrielle cleared her throat, uncertain she could speak without her voice quavering while the darkly handsome—utterly impertinent—stranger moved his gaze over her, his tactile perusal irking her as much as it was inflaming her. And that irked her further still.

"It's all right, Aubert," she said to the servant. With a nod, the majordomo bowed and left the study.

He found you! She cursed her luck. And here she thought it was still on her side. The entire ride home, she'd checked repeatedly to see if they were being followed.

There had been no sign of him.

He was far cleverer than she'd given him credit for. Damn him. And his physical allure.

"You look better in this attire than the one you had on last night," he said with a hint of a smile on his gorgeous mouth.

Caroline and Bernadette moved close to her.

Placing a hand on her arm, Caroline asked *sotto voce*, "Is this the 'small problem' you mentioned earlier?"

"Good Lord, there's nothing small about the man," Bernadette whispered, eyeing him.

Gabrielle took a deep breath and let it out slowly, striving for a level of composure she didn't feel inside. Dealing with the intrusive male in her study was more than enough, without her friends adding to the challenge. "Enough. Not another word from either of you." Her voice was soft but firm. She didn't want them giving this man any information about her or them. "Ladies, please excuse us. I have a word or two to say to our *visitor*," she remarked louder, holding his gaze firmly.

"Alone? In private?" Caroline asked, her unease tingeing her tone.

"Yes. Please leave now." Out of the corner of her eye, Gabrielle saw her two friends exchange concerned looks, but without further ado, they dropped their gazes as they passed the man standing in the room, and exited the study, closing the door quietly behind them.

"How did you find me?" She didn't waste a moment's time getting to the point.

He cocked his head, a lock of dark hair falling across his brow, looking ever so appealing. "I followed you."

"Why? What on earth are you doing here?"

"I felt a visit was in order."

Her brows shot up. "*A visit?* Are you entirely well in the mind? What about our encounter would have made you think I would want a visit from you?"

A smile tugged at the corners of his mouth. He approached, stopping before her. Towering over her. Yet she refused to step back, or do anything to indicate in any way she was unsettled by him.

"You asked what I was doing here and I responded. You never asked if I thought you'd like a visit from me."

Her ire mounted by the moment—thanks to his unmitigated gall, the smug look in those light-colored eyes.

And his wonderful scent.

Though she couldn't quite describe it, it was tantalizing in the extreme. She actually had the maddening urge to lean in and inhale deeply.

"The point to you being here is?" she pressed. Dear God, how she wanted him to leave. She didn't know what to make of his unprecedented effect on her. Or how to control it.

He was making her feel dread, and heaven help her . . . desire. Seducing her senses in a way no other man ever had.

She wasn't at all like some of her half sisters. She wasn't the type of woman who became giddy over a handsome face.

"First, allow me to properly introduce myself," he said. "My name is Mathias de Tesson, Marquis de Montfort. And you are?"

She simply glared back at him.

He lifted a brow. "Not going to answer?"

Damned pushy man. "No."

"Fine. Then I shall tell you what I know." He folded his hands behind his back and slowly strolled around her. "I know who owns this townhouse, the Marquis de Gaillard. I know he's got quite a reputation when it comes to keeping mistresses. He maintains a number of them at any given time. His favorite is with him at his château as we speak." He stopped behind her. His body was so close to hers. A luscious heat emanated from him, inciting a quickening low in her belly. He leaned in, his mouth all but touching her ear. "This very townhouse is one he offered to a former mistress, one whom he's since tired of," he said softly, his warm breath caressing her skin, sending a ripple of heat down her spine. She barely held back the shiver. "You have a wealthy benefactor. You don't need the coin. Or to venture out in the middle of the night as you did to play Basset. Why were you there last eve—dressed as a man?"

Gabrielle didn't respond. She was working too hard at keeping her breathing even. The information about her philandering uncle wasn't new. Her reactions to this man were. Her nipples were hard. Her senses were awake and highly attuned to him. Reacting to any and every small thing he did.

"Still no answer?" This time his lips brushed her ear. She jumped and spun around. His slight touch shot a bolt of sensations right down to her feminine core. Startling her.

"This may come as a complete shock to you, given your staggering audacity, but I owe you no explanations or answers," she tried saying with finality, but wasn't sure she'd succeeded; the light throbbing between her legs was a horrible distraction.

Her treacherous body was behaving in the unruliest way.

"Are you going to be there on Saturday?" he asked.

"Yes."

"That's the wrong answer. Stay home."

"No." She uttered the word firmly. Could he tell the frenzy he'd caused inside her?

"I could tell the Duc about you, you know. That you are a woman."

The last thing she needed was to pique anyone else's interest, but she didn't cave in to threats. Others had tried to coerce her at court.

With no success.

Gabrielle collected herself and schooled her features. Affecting her usual blasé tone, she said, "Do you think he'd care? I don't. I got the distinct impression his only concern was recouping his losses and perhaps winning some coin from me."

She'd done it. She'd successfully countered his threat and taken the life out of it. It was visible on his face.

He sighed and rested his hands on his hips. "Look, believe it or not, I came here because I am trying to help you."

That inspired a laugh. "Help me? I won a considerable sum last night, while you lost half your winnings. What help do I need from you?" She didn't wait for him to respond. "You and I both know why you're here. Clearly you've nothing better to do with your time than to poke your nose where it doesn't belong. And when you learned who owned this home, you of course thought, 'poor lonely mistress, so neglected by her lover.' Naturally she would eagerly allow you a tumble. Isn't that so?"

She was livid—with herself for reacting so strongly to someone who was of no importance to her. And for not putting on a convincing enough performance last night. Though she didn't think she'd failed miserably at behaving like a male, having this man see through her disguise clearly proved otherwise.

The only thing that gave her any pleasure was that he was so far off course with his belief that she was the Marquis de Gaillard's mistress.

He stepped close to her. She stepped back, something she hadn't meant to do, a knee-jerk reaction on her part that made her want to kick herself. It showed weakness.

He advanced another step and slipped his fingers under her chin. She couldn't back away this time, even if she wanted to. She'd backed up against the tall marble table in the room.

"If you're asking if I want you, the answer is yes. I won't deny it. What man wouldn't want you? In fact, if truth be told, I spent all last night thinking about tasting every inch of your edible form." Her sex clenched.

He leaned in, his solid body pressing so delectably against hers. She leaned back away from the lure of his mouth and gripped the edge of the table. "Can you feel how hard you make me? What you do to me?"

Her heart pounded. How could anyone possibly miss *that*? The stiff bulge inside his breeches pressed against her belly and made the bud between her legs throb harder.

"I see what I do to you, too, beautiful Snow Princess."

At the word "princess," she flinched.

He didn't seem to notice and continued. "So very alluring, yet with a haughty veneer. I see through that icy exterior of yours," he said. "I see a beautiful, naturally sensuous woman. I see the way her body reacts to me. You know as well as I do any carnal encounter between us would be heated, delicious, and intense."

No one had ever spoken to her like this. Other men had made comments about her physical appeal. She'd always dismissed them as empty compliments, as the flattery was only offered in front of the King. She should have done the same with what Mathias was saying, but instead, the look in his eyes, the low timbre of his voice, and his hot hard body pressed against hers made it impossible.

And thrilling.

She swallowed twice before she could say, "St-step back, please."

To her surprise, he complied, promptly. She suddenly found him a good two feet from her, his hands back on his hips.

She hadn't expected immediate compliance. Though she didn't think he'd force himself on her, she thought she'd have to insist.

He was forever doing the unexpected.

To her chagrin, without the heat and press of his body against hers, she actually felt *bereft*.

"If you're not going to tell me anything about yourself, tell me your name." The most gorgeous, smile appeared on his face. "Then I'll at least have a name to put to the woman I've been fantasizing about."

Thankfully, he hasn't been able to learn your identity. But then again, who would, or could tell him? No one knew she was here, except her uncle, and he was presently a distance away. She was careful not to venture out into the city where she might be recognized, unless in disguise. And then there were the servants. Her uncle paid them well. They knew to hold their tongues or lose their employment.

Gabrielle decided to change tactics. Holding her silence was only fueling his curiosity about her. She'd toss him a bone.

"Well?" he prompted.

"Silvie," slipped past her lips. It was the first name that entered her mind and the very last one she should have offered *him*. She mentally chastised herself for choosing *that* name. Of her many given names, that was the one her mother, Daniel, and at times even Bernadette and Caroline called her. Only those closest to her used it.

But never in the presence of the King. His Majesty didn't care for it.

"Silvie?" He said her name with a weighty skepticism, as though he didn't believe her. "Silvie what?"

Fool, now that you've offered the name, you can't exactly change it, can you? "Just Silvie."

"All right, just Silvie, what were you doing at the gaming den, dressed as a man?"

"I was doing what everyone else was doing at the gaming den. Playing Basset. I like the thrill of the game. It's exciting. And I dressed the way I dressed because I didn't want anyone to recognize me, *obviously*." She sharpened her tone, hoping he'd tire of her coarseness and leave her be.

"I don't believe you, Silvie. There is much more to all this than you are saying." He stepped close again but this time he gently cupped her cheek. "There is more to you than you allow others to see. Behind the tall thick wall where you conceal yourself is the real woman. One I'd very much like to know."

No man had ever dared touch her the way this man did. Worse, she liked the way he was touching her. The way his body had felt against hers. Too much.

"Please heed my warning, beautiful Silvie. Don't go to Navers's gaming den on Saturday. For if you do, there will be consequences you don't wish to face."

He stepped back, kissed her hand, then bade her a good night, and walked out of the room, leaving her body heated, trembling from the inside out, and her mind spinning from his ominous parting words.

*****

"Where have you been?" Valette rose from his chair in Mathias's library. He'd just returned home, only to be informed by his majordomo that the sergeant was here and had insisted on waiting for his return.

The man irked him. There was nothing he liked about the single-minded civil servant.

"I don't believe I owe you a moment-by-moment accounting of my time. Do remember your place." He didn't normally stand on ceremony, but this man had the most boorish manners.

Mathias's senior by at least five ten years, Valette had small dark eyes and a long nose that reminded him of a rodent.

"We are supposed to be working on the Duc's private gambling den together," Valette said.

"No, I'm supposed to be working on it. You're supposed to be assisting."

"Yes, well, there were twenty men there last night. You've only given me the names of seven. We'll need the rest."

There were nineteen men there last night—and one very beautiful, very obstinate woman.

"I'm to be reporting on the goings on," Mathias corrected him. "I've already indicated how the Duc is advancing funds to those whose luck has turned, keeping them in the game, driving up their debt and taking lands, horses, anything of value from them, assisting them all the way to their ruin."

"Yes. True." Valette scratched his head. "That has already been reported back to the Lieutenant General of Police. However, as pleased as he is with the information you've provided thus far, he needs to know who attends the games."

"Not everyone. Just the regulars. That is my objective."

He wished he knew why Silvie, if that was even her real name, showed up at the Duc's Basset table. The reason was much more involved than she wanted to admit.

She was being secretive. *Merde*. The more she withheld, the more she spiked his interest. He could tell there were many layers to this fascinating woman. He wanted to peel them all away. He was too intrigued by her, and he wanted her too damned much. The Marquis de Gaillard was a colossal fool to have abandoned this particular mistress.

He didn't deserve her.

Clearly, he didn't favor her, and Mathias had no qualms poaching. But Silvie would require a slow seduction. Something he was not used to.

He wasn't accustomed to having to work at landing a woman in his bed. Yet with this woman, every fiber of his being told him she'd be worth the effort and the wait.

In the meantime, he prayed she'd heed his warning and remain home Saturday night.

The last thing he wanted was to have her become a regular at the Duc's Basset tables.

CHAPTER FOUR

Gabrielle walked into the Duc de Navers's private gaming den, feeling confident. All day she'd sequestered herself in her private apartments away from Caroline and Bernadette, and worked on bolstering her confidence and courage. And wrestling the far too distracting Marquis de Montfort from her thoughts.

Honing her focus.

She could do this. She could. She *would* win back the rest of Daniel's debt.

And she'd be damned if she was going to let Montfort scare her away. No one rattled her. Not even the King of the most powerful nation in all of Christendom.

No one was going to keep her from doing what she needed to do.

Montfort may be gorgeous, and maddeningly seductive, but he was also overbearing, pushy. And annoying beyond words.

It was bad enough he had followed her, showed up at her home, dictated to her, and aroused her body.

Now he'd even muscled his way into her dreams. She was having carnal dreams about the man that were become more and more heated. Erotic dreams in which he was doing more than just caressing her hand or cheek. He'd stoked her body, in places no man had ever touched. They were so vivid, she could feel the warmth and texture of his skin against hers. The sumptuous press of his hard body. And the score of his fingers over her sensitive sex. Gabrielle woke up each morning her sex aching and mortifyingly wet.

As if she didn't have enough on her mind. Thanks to Montfort, her thoughts now wavered between the diamonds tucked under her mattress, and fantasizing about a certain the Marquis on it.

She'd never had a lover. Never been with a man. Never found any at court particularly stirring. And yet, Montfort was beyond stirring. He was wreaking havoc on her mind and body.

Glancing about the Duc's drawing room, she noted that there were fewer people in attendance this eve.

The same three tables were set. She strode to the same chair she'd used last time. It had been lucky. And she had to maintain the luck she'd had the last time. Over last few days she'd observed men in a way she'd never done before, both the male servants and the men on the street below her window. She studied their walk. Their mannerisms. Practiced mimicking them.

She wanted no one else guessing her gender.

Ignoring how itchy her periwig was, she cast another furtive glance about. No Montfort. Could it be that the obnoxious man wasn't showing up tonight? Could she be that fortunate?

The banker sat down, joining the other four players at the table. Gabrielle pulled out her pouch of *louis d'or*. She had two pouches on her. One with the diamonds and another with half the winnings from the previous night. Thankfully, she didn't need to risk the diamonds tonight. She'd brought them strictly for luck. Tucked in her pocket, they'd brought her great fortune last time.

God help her, she needed more of the same tonight.

Half her winnings from the previous game was still a handsome sum and more than enough to win back the balance of her brother's losings.

The banker began dealing out thirteen cards per player. It was then she heard the door open and close behind her. A figure approached the table and sat down in the vacant chair across from her.

She didn't need to look up. Her nerve endings tingled, already keenly aware of the identity of the newly arrived player. Dragging her gaze up, praying her senses were wrong, she was immediately captured in a pair of light gray eyes.

Montfort.

He didn't look as though he was happy to see her. Good. The feeling was mutual. *Liar*, her body screamed. It was at-ingle. *And a traitor*. Gabrielle fought back the urge to gnash her teeth.

A strong hand gripped her shoulder, yanking her focus up. She found Navers smiling down at her. "Welcome back," he said, seating himself beside the banker. It was obvious he intended to assist him by being the game's *croupière* again.

She responded with a nod.

"Let us begin." Navers's comment was to the group. "Place your bets."

Gabrielle turned up four cards and placed three *louis d'or* on each, trying to ignore Montfort and her racing heart. She hadn't been this discomposed the last time. Mathias was making her nervous—worse than before.

Forget him. Stay focused.

The banker dealt a ten and then a five.

She'd won her *couch*.

Joy and confidence shot through her system. Her nerves dissolved and she relaxed her shoulders. She couldn't help but glance up at Montfort and had to fight back her smile. He'd won his *couch* as well. It delighted her. Not because she cared whether he won or not. What made her happy was that the very same thing happened the last time when she'd had such enormous luck.

They'd both won their *couch* on the first deal.

It was a good sign. One that suggested good fortune was on her side—that a repeat of what happened the other night was about to happen again. Substantial winnings awaited her this night.

There had to be.

Not wanting to do anything to disrupt something as fickle and fleeting as luck, she echoed her pattern of play, doing everything exactly the same as she'd done before. Crooking the corner of her card, she indicated she was going on for a higher payout. She was going for a *sept-et-le-va*—a chance at winning seven times her bet. It was a daring play that had paid off the last time, and in fact, many times in the past.

The banker turned up his card. However, this time her winning card didn't show up. She watched as he took her money.

Her gaze drifted to Montfort. His expression was unreadable but his winnings were clear. He'd played it safer and won another couch.

It's all right. It's a loss, but you'll win it back. The night was young and she still had plenty of money left.

Less than an hour later, she was down to her last few *louis d'or*. Her palms were sweaty. Her heart galloped and her head was horribly itchy from the cursed periwig.

She'd lost almost every coin she'd brought with her.

Montfort, on the other hand, was untroubled. Why should he be? He had a good-sized stack of gold coins before him.

Her luck would turn for the better. Good fortune had been missing all night and was due to show up. She wasn't going to panic. Nor dwell on how much she'd lost. Turning up two cards, she placed her final coins on them.

The banker dealt his cards. "King wins. Knave loses."

To her horror, her money was swept up by the Duc. *Oh God!* She could barely breathe. She'd lost it all. Half of what she'd previously won for Daniel.

"Sir, are you listening?" The Duc's voice jolted her out of her whirling thoughts. Quickly she realized he was speaking to her.

"Pardon?" she asked.

"I said, are you going to make another bet?"

All she had on her to bet with were her diamonds. She needed one good win to turn things around. Dare she try? One player at the table had already bet everything he owned and lost. She'd watched, sick to her stomach as he was forced to sign over his château and hôtel. The other players at the table rose and left, all considerably lighter in the purse, but at least they still owed their homes.

She and Montfort were the only players remaining at their table.

Knowing the odds were better with fewer players in the game, she made up her mind to play on.

Did she really have a choice?

Deciding she'd risk only one diamond, she reached inside her breast pocket and pulled out the pouch of diamonds, praying no one could see how her hands trembled. Somehow she got her fingers to work and not fumble while loosening the ties.

Gabrielle pulled out a diamond and set it down on her card.

"Not enough," Navers said.

Gabrielle frowned. "What do you mean? The diamond is worth at least six hundred *louis d'or.*"

"The stakes are higher than that. You bet at least two or you don't play."

A small voice whispered, *Walk away.* But she quashed the voice. She couldn't win if she didn't play.

Gabrielle pulled out a second diamond and set it down on her card.

Montfort placed his bet on his own cards.

With trepidation in her heart and her stomach queasy, she turned and watched the banker's hands as he flipped two cards over. "Ten wins. Eight loses."

As fast as that, her diamonds were taken away.

She was shaking and pulled her gaze up from the empty spot that once had her precious gems to Montfort. He'd won a *sept-et-le-va*.

"I'll take payment in diamonds as well as coin." Montfort astonished her with his request. "It will save you the trouble of having to deal with the gems, Navers," he added.

The Duc thought for a moment then waved someone over. A man about Navers's age had been standing in the corner of the room the entire time observing the goings-on. He approached. Like the Duc, he wasn't wearing a mask.

"Check the diamonds," the Duc ordered him. Pulling out an eyepiece from inside his justacorps, the man examined both gems.

"The bigger one is worth about six hundred *louis d'or*," he advised Navers. "And the smaller of the two, about four hundred."

With a nod from Navers to the banker, the banker pushed her diamonds and the balance of Montfort's winnings toward him. Frozen in disbelief, she watched helplessly as Montfort scooped up his winnings, dropped them into a pouch, and quit the game.

In moments, he was out the door with the King's precious gems.

On shaky legs she rose, murmured she'd had enough, and walked across the drawing room, forcing herself to keep to a swift walk and not break into a full-out run after Montfort.

The instant she made it to the hallway, she tore after the man with her diamonds.

*****

Mathias stopped short in front of his carriage and raked a hand though his hair.

Merde!

He fucking hated seeing the Comte de Rochemore lose everything. This was the first time since Victor's death he'd seen a loss of that magnitude. *Jésus-Christ*, the man had four daughters! He'd never come up with a dowry for them now. Tonight he'd sealed their fate. There would be no marriages. No children. For any of them. All four young women would have no choice but to enter a convent and live out the remainder of their days in the cloister.

Whether they wished it or not.

Curling his fingers, Mathias let loose a string of expletives. He was so overwrought, he wanted to slam his fist into something. Anything.

This game had to stop. He wanted it to stop. It was leveling the lives of so many innocent people—people who'd never sat at a Basset table. He thought when Sard had approached him, this would be easy.

It was gut-wrenching.

He'd started all this for Victor, thinking this was the least he could do for him. After watching Rochemore sink farther and farther into debt at the Basset table tonight, he decided he'd done enough for his friend.

Victor could have done a million things differently, not the least of which was having the courage to deal with the aftermath of his financial losses.

Instead, he'd chosen to abandon his wife and child after he'd driven them into poverty.

Fuck. He was tired of torturing himself over Victor's death. Tired of wondering if he could have done more. Seen more sooner. He'd spent months letting it eat at him. It was Victor who should be the one consoling his wife and child.

He should never have left his family to fend for themselves, destitute.

Mathias had stepped forward and purchased a townhouse in the city for Victor's wife Marie and son, so they'd have a home to live in. He even gave Marie a monthly allowance.

He was sick to death of the weight he felt in his chest over Victor's untimely death. And he'd done everything he could to make matters right. Including doing something he thought he'd never do again—enter another gaming den.

Tomorrow he had another meeting with that weasel Valette, and would have to give up more names.

Which brought him to a different dilemma. Silvie. A willful woman who didn't have enough good sense to walk away from a losing table.

He'd had to watch that damned fiasco, too. Her tension and horror mounted with each hand she lost. He didn't want to sense it. Or notice it at all. Yet he was maddeningly attuned to her every emotion tonight—and the carnal hunger he felt for her.

She had him utterly enthralled at every level. He wanted her so badly, his sac ached.

This attraction to her was the last thing he damned well needed.

Especially when he was an informant for the King's Lieutenant General of Police on a mission to report the names of those who regularly frequented Navers's gaming den. He wanted to do just that—and be done with the matter.

But this mysterious woman was convoluting matters considerably.

Worse still, she was playing games—beyond Basset—and he had no idea why. He didn't know what to make of her secrets. He didn't know how to snap the fascination. Or mute the sexual pull between them. He couldn't stop thinking about her. Or the memory of her heated reactions to his touch. He'd spent the better part of the last few days and nights at a cock-stand for a female he wanted to protect. And who wanted no advice or protection from him.

Isn't that fucking perfect?

He couldn't very well tell her the details of his mission—especially to a woman he knew nothing about. And he certainly couldn't seem to impress on her to stay away from Navers's hôtel.

"Montfort!" A female voice grabbed his attention. He turned around and saw Silvie racing toward him. He knew it was only a matter of time before she came after him. He had her gems, after all. They were important to her. The devastation in her eyes when she'd lost them was impossible to miss.

She stopped before him, her breathing quick. "I need to speak to you," she said.

"Yes, well, I need to shake you for your fool-headed play. What did you think you were doing in there? I thought you had some experience in the game. You don't stay and continue to lose money when you've no luck on your side to speak of!"

She lowered her eyes. "Yes, you're right, of course." Her response was soft, her manner demure. And he was stunned. Since when did this woman become so docile?

"I really must speak to you," she repeated and looked around. They were alone in the courtyard, save for the horses and the drivers. "But not here. Come to my townhouse. Tonight. I'll meet you there."

With that she stalked away briskly.

Mathias was drained and angry and, now thanks to her, his cock was hard again.

For a woman in men's clothing.

Before Victor took his own life, Mathias had a normal existence. He attended the theater, was welcomed in all the best Salons in Paris, and actually had women who gave him their name as well as their bodies. And yet here he was, covertly working to topple a Duc and turn in his peers, all the while panting after another man's mistress who was cloaked in secrecy. If he had any good sense at all, he'd get in his carriage and go home, but wild horses couldn't keep him from Silvie's townhouse or from hearing what she had to tell him.

He was going to demystify this mystifying beauty and get her out of his system.

This wasn't going to get any more involved than it already was.

CHAPTER FIVE

The moment Mathias arrived at Silvie's townhouse, he was asked by the majordomo to follow him.

As the man led him across the grand vestibule, Mathias tried his level best to learn the name of the lady of the house from the servant. To learn how long she'd been living in the townhouse. Hell, to learn anything about her at all. Although no one else seemed to know anything about the Marquis de Gaillard's new mistress, surely the majordomo did.

It proved to be a futile exercise.

The blasted somber servant was tight-lipped.

As soon as they began climbing the stairs, Mathias realized he wasn't heading to a drawing room. *Dieu.* He was being led to her private apartments.

His greedy cock thickened farther and strained harder against the inside of his breeches. *Easy now.* He never knew what to expect with this woman. She wasn't the most predictable of females. He wasn't about to make any assumptions.

Reaching one of the doors in the corridor, the servant knocked and opened it upon hearing his mistress's bidding.

Mathias stepped in. The servant closed the door behind him leaving Mathias standing in an antechamber. He looked around. The sitting room had chairs of light blue damask and gold and white walls. But the room was empty.

"In here, please," he heard her say from the bedchamber.

His heart began to race. *Merde.* He was acting as if he was some nervous youth about to fuck his first woman.

He entered the bedchamber and found her standing near the large four-poster bed. She was in a rich red and white gown, her hair in a gorgeous cascade of dark curls reaching her shoulders.

She was nothing short of breathtaking.

Dressed in feminine attire that showed off her fine female attributes, she made his knees weak. What was conspicuously absent was her jewelry. She wore none.

She'd had on a few fine pieces the other day, so he knew she owned some. In no way was he going to presume it was omitted on purpose because she anticipated sex and didn't want it getting in the way.

Mathias was going to let her take the initial lead, then take over, moving one slow seductive step at a time.

In her bedchamber, alone with her, mere feet from her bed, he'd do absolutely nothing that would jeopardize this moment.

She had her hands folded before her. He watched as she smoothed her skirts and refolded them. *She's nervous. All the more reason to take it slow.*

"Thank you for coming," she said.

"You're welcome." He offered nothing more, but simply waited for her next words. Her next move.

She smoothed her skirts again and paused, almost as though she was grappling with her next words. Finally she said, "I find myself in a bit of a situation."

"Oh? And what situation is that?"

She bit her lush bottom lip and dropped her gaze to the floor briefly before she lifted her chin, looked him straight in the eye, and said, "I need my diamonds back."

Mathias held his tongue. Any response and she likely wouldn't elaborate. He wanted her as much as he wanted to know about her.

For the life of him, he couldn't understand what all the secrecy was about. Why the desire to disguise herself?

He doubted Gaillard cared a whit if his mistress played some Basset—illegal or not. And if he were willing to provide her with a lavish home such as this, he'd likely be inclined to cover any of her losses.

His silence worked. She continued. "The diamonds are . . . very important to me, you see. I cannot lose them. I am willing to compensate you for them."

His groin tightened. Every fiber in his being anticipated exactly what compensation she was offering. Still he kept silent.

His gaze dropped to her hands. He noted she was clutching them tightly. *Dieu*, he knew the diamonds were important to her, but he hadn't anticipated her being in such distress over them. It was palpable.

"If . . ." She stopped and started anew. "You give me back my diamonds and I'll . . . rather . . ."

Out with it, Gabrielle, she told herself and pushed the rest of the words off her tongue. "I'll be . . . yours for the night."

The flare of hot interest in his eyes made her sex clench. All right. She'd admit it. She was hardly being the sacrificial lamb here.

You know as well as I do any carnal encounter between us would be heated, delicious, and intense. His words had been haunting her for days and even more so at night.

The King would select her husband soon. She'd heard that copulation with a husband for the purposes of procreation was entirely different from sex with a lover. Before she was married to a man who would likely ship her off to some isolated château, she wanted to know what it would be like to couple with a man who heated her blood the way this man did.

She'd never met anyone like him. As it was, he was making her pulse race just by his presence.

The more she'd contemplated the proposition on the way home, the more it held appeal. She'd enjoy an amorous encounter, experience firsthand some of the physical pleasure she'd heard about, and gain back her diamonds.

The benefit to her was twofold.

Slowly, he approached, all that tall strong masculine beauty coming her way. Gripped by anticipation, her insides quivered.

He stopped before her, forcing her to lift her chin in order to look him in the eye. Dear God, how she loved his height. No, more than just his height. There was so much about him that she found physically appealing. His gaze dipped briefly down to her décolletage, her nipples hardening at the mere glance.

He slipped his fingers under her chin, leaned in, and slowly grazed his lips up the side of her neck. She closed her eyes, her breathing instantly quickening. The sensations felt so good, so decadent. It rippled all the way down to her toes.

"You're going to let me have you any way I want?" he murmured in her ear.

There were different ways? "Yes . . ."

"And you want two diamonds for your body . . . for one night?" Ever so lightly, his hot mouth retraced its tantalizing path back down her neck to the curve of her shoulder.

"*Hmm?* Oh, yes . . . two . . ." She licked her lips. "Both diamonds." This was so much better than anything anyone had described.

Lifting his head, he hauled her up against him and claimed her mouth, his tongue driving past her lips on her gasp. She fisted his justacorps and held on as his tongue swirled and stroked hers with mind-spinning intensity. He tasted so good. No, he tasted better than good. Better than anything she'd ever known. Hungry for more, she matched him stroke for stroke with the same famished zeal. She'd never been kissed before, never knew a man this exhilarating. She rubbed herself against the hard bulge pushing against her belly. His groan spiked her need and moistened her sex, the light pulsing between her legs growing stronger with each skillful sweep of his tongue. She'd no idea how he had the ability to awaken her long-dormant body, to set every nerve ending quivering with excitement.

He broke the kiss sooner than she wanted. A protest escaped her throat. She snapped her eyes open, her breathing sharp and shallow, and there, in those sensual light-colored eyes, was the very same hot need scorching through her blood.

The sight weakened her knees.

"Wh-What say you, Mathias? Do we have a bargain?" She was dying to touch his skin. To explore every inch of his powerfully sculpted physique.

No, more than that. She was dying to know the feel of him inside her, their bodies joined in a lovers' embrace, a connection she'd never craved before.

He cupped her breast and rubbed his thumb across her distended nipple through her clothing. His rhythmic strokes over the sensitized peak made her shiver, the sensations lancing into her core. She had to swallow down a moan.

"Ah yes, the bargain . . ." The sweet torment on her nipple was driving her to distraction.

"*Yes?*" she prompted, desperate to get on with it. "What's your answer? What do you say?"

"I say . . ." He dropped his hand away. "I don't pay for sex. Ever." With a turn of his heel, he started toward the door.

In her heated haze, it took a moment for his words to register in her mind. Her heart lurched. She raced up and jumped into his path, stopping his progress.

"Surely you jest! You're not actually leaving?"

She sensed his anger and struggled with what to do. What words would convince him to stay? He couldn't leave her like this. She wanted him so badly, it hurt.

"When a woman gives herself to me, it's for one reason. *Only* one reason. Because she wants to." He reached inside his dark gray justacorps, pulled out a small pouch, and tossed it onto the side table beside them. Next thing she knew, he was lifting her off the floor, as if she weighed nothing at all, and set her bottom down on the side table, too.

"You want your diamonds? Here are your diamonds." He picked up the pouch beside her and shoved it into her hand. "Open it. They're both in there."

She loosened the ties to the dark blue velvet pouch and peered in. Just as he'd said; the King's diamonds were indeed both there. She closed up the pouch and met his gaze, perplexed.

"You're going to just give them back to me? Without any compensation of any kind?" Her body screamed, *No! Take me!*

"They are yours. No conditions attached."

"But . . . But you could have used these as leverage, to force me to—"

"Give me sex as well as information about you? I'm quite aware of that. I won't use coercion. What you give me is going to be of your own free will."

She was astounded and moved beyond words. She didn't know any man who wouldn't have used the situation to his advantage. No man she knew would have returned the diamonds without making some sort of demand for some kind of gain. His gesture was generous and touching and for the first time she saw him in a totally different light.

It made her want him more.

He pulled the pouch from her hands and dropped it beside her on the wooden surface. Setting his palms on her knees, he gently spread them apart and stepped between them, his actions taking her by surprise. A thrill shot up her spine.

With her legs apart, she was all too aware of his proximity to her slick sex, aching to be filled.

He gripped her bottom and pulled her tightly against him, her sex coming in quick contact with the bulge in his breeches. She gasped, their clothing muting none of the delicious sensation. He then rolled his hips, plying the most exquisite pressure. She lost her breath and grabbed his sleeves, the bud between her legs now throbbing fiercely.

"You don't have the diamonds to hide behind any longer," he said, his mouth so temptingly close to her own. "So if you want me to take you, you're going to have to admit to it. Ask for it. What is it going to be, Silvie? Are you going to give yourself to me?"

Her sex answered with a warm gush. She wanted him to be the one to introduce her to carnal delights.

In her life she'd never wanted anything more.

Her hands flew to the front of her gown. Feeling his heated gaze on her all the while, she quickly opened the fastenings and slipped off her sleeves. She attacked the stays next, spreading and pulling, her breaths ragged, her fingers fumbling, eager to free herself from the confines of her clothing for him.

She wasn't in the least bit embarrassed by having him see her in a state of undress. Not when she was burning for him, her clothes feeling hot and suffocating.

Not when she had to have him or die.

Seeing her struggling, he lent an expert hand here and there until he finally pulled off her gown and tossed it to the floor, then stepped back in between her opened thighs.

He slipped his hand under her knee-length chemise and brushed the heel of his palm against her mound. She jerked at the decadent sensation.

His smile broadened as he loosened the ties to her caleçons, then cupped her sex. The heat radiating from his hand through her drawers was melting her mind. He began massaging her slick sex through the fabric. She gripped his shoulders tightly and bit her lip, trying to keep down her whimpers and soft moans, without success, her mewls punctuating the silence in the room.

"Your drawers are wet," he said, seemingly pleased by it.

It wasn't something she could control. It was what he did to her.

He slid the drawers off her, too, followed quickly by her garters, stockings, and shoes.

By the time she was down to just her chemise, her fever had reached an unbearable pitch. Always guarded and reserved, it felt wonderful to be this unbridled. Unrestrained. Her life a stifling existence, she'd found a new freedom—all due to a man who incited her senses like no other.

He pulled off the last article of clothing and let it drop to the floor. There was something wicked and thrilling about being naked before him while he was still fully dressed. She watched his gaze move over her form with male appreciation. It fluttered her stomach.

"You're so very beautiful," he said, caressing the back of his fingers between her breasts, gliding them down to her quivering belly. Dipping his fingers into her sex, past her soaked curls, he captured her clitoris and gave it light pinch. She practically shot up off the side table as a cry left her throat, the sensations sending her rushing headlong toward a precipice. She was about to hurl over it when he released his hold on the throbbing bud and removed his hand. By the smile on his face, she could tell he'd purposely stopped her from falling over the edge. She squeaked out in frustration.

"I knew you'd be as fiery in the boudoir as you are out of it. Beautiful Snow Princess, I like how you melt for me." He rested his hands on the tops of her thigh, his thumbs so close to her needy sex. "Ask for it, Silvie. Let me hear the words from that pretty mouth. Ask for it and I'll give you what you want."

She was quaking both inside and out. "I want you to . . . Will you . . . Take me." She couldn't catch her breath.

Still with a devilish smile, he removed his justacorps, his vest, and opened up his breeches. "With pleasure." His voice was so low and sinfully sensual as he pulled out his shirttails and yanked the linen shirt off, too, sending it to the floor to join the rest of the clothing.

His solid chest was bare. She drank in its chiseled perfection, moving her gaze down over his muscled belly all the way to his sex boldly jutting out of his breeches. Once, not long ago, she'd had a glimpse of an erotic illustration. She'd even seen nudes in murals and art, but never the male anatomy up close.

Gabrielle reached out, her hands trembling slightly, and ran them over the dips and ripples of his chest and abdomen, his skin warm beneath her touch, under her hand his heart beating quickly, racing her own.

Taking her hand, he brought it to his shaft. Immediately, she curled her fingers around his hard length, reveling in his groan. She luxuriated over the feel of him in her hand, riveted by the pleasure etched across his handsome features as he moved her fist up to the engorged head and down to the base with long unhurried strokes. The proportions of his sex were as impressive as the rest of him. It was inebriating to watch him, to stroke him. To pleasure him.

"I've been fantasizing about you since we met. Dreaming of all the ways I'm going to fuck you." Dipping his head, he brushed his mouth against her lips. "How do you want to be taken, Silvie?" he whispered. "Fast, or slow?"

She couldn't stop stroking him.

"Yes." She parted her lips for him, eager to have him in her mouth.

"Yes to which?" His mouth teasingly hovered over hers.

"Yes to all of it. Both. However you want. Just do it now."

Softly, he chuckled. Removing her hand from his sex, he stripped off the remainder of his clothing.

This time he spread her legs a little wider when he stepped in between.

"The bed is over there," she said, stating the obvious, her senses in a frenzy, desperately trying to move things along.

He pulled her up against him, her soaked sex kissing his shaft. The slightest smile played on his beautiful mouth.

"I've been hard for you for days," he said, stroking his erection against her slickened folds. "You're going to take my cock right here, Silvie." He kissed her mouth, her jaw, the sensitive spot below her ear. "We'll use the bed next time." With that, he lowered his head and sucked her nipple into his hot mouth. She cried out and thrust her hips hard against him, a completely reflexive response. Unfazed by her eruptive reaction, he leaned her back, the back of her head pressing against the wall while his mouth sucked and savored her nipple. Alternating between breasts, he gave each sensitive tip its due carnal care until he had her writhing and panting. A fresh rush of warm wetness flowed from her core onto his hard cock pressed so firmly against her folds.

He groaned. "I love that . . ." He lightly bit her nipple; she held his head to her and whimpered. "I love how you're creaming on my cock." Raising his head, he wrapped her legs around his waist and possessed her mouth with a kiss. It was demanding, hot and delectably fierce.

He gripped her hips. Then his cock was wedged firmly against her opening. Her heart hammered. Her body celebrated. At last! Joy and pleasure swamping her senses. She wiggled and squirmed, gluttonous for more.

"Easy, *chère*," he rasped against her mouth. "I know you're eager. Allow me."

She grasped his shoulders, just as he drove forward. A sudden sharp pain made her recoil and cry out.

"*Jésus-Christ!*" exploded from his lips, his shock evident on his face. He'd only penetrated her partway, her body shaking with a mixture of pain and pleasure.

Her need was still a strong undercurrent through it all.

He started to pull out.

"No!" She tightened her legs around his waist, the sudden movement causing him to sink an inch deeper. His growl eclipsed her moan. No pain this time. Just a delicious stretching. She drew her arms around him. "Don't stop." She rained kisses on his mouth, his face, his neck, famished for his taste. For him. "Please . . . give me more . . ." Already the discomfort had receded, overshadowed by the agony of her unfulfilled desire. Her core was pulsing hungrily, his partial possession maddening. She wanted all of him. Tentatively, she moved her hips, trying to take him in.

"Merde . . ." He tightened his grip her hips, stilling her. The muscles in his shoulders tight and tense beneath her hands, he rested his forehead against hers, his breathing as labored as her own. She could tell he was grappling with what to do, given his discovery of her virginity.

"I want you, Mathias . . . Please, don't stop. Not now. It doesn't hurt anymore . . . Take me . . . I want more . . ." She couldn't believe what was tumbling from her mouth. She never spoke of her needs and wants. Not ever.

Impatient, she tightened her arms and legs around him and tried to move her hips again, an awkward, unpracticed movement that garnered her only a small measure of success. Frustration erupted out of her.

Another oath slipped softly from his lips. "All right, Silvie . . . Loosen your legs. Let me give you more." He slipped his hands under her bottom the moment she complied and lifted her into his plunge, burying his cock into her with a single luscious glide.

Her head fell back, a soft sound of pleasure leaving her lungs. Oh God . . . He was so deep. She felt so full. There was no pain, just pure pleasure. It felt better than anything she could have imagined. It felt *incredible*.

"How's that? You like that, Silvie?" he asked, his voice gruff with desire. "You want more?"

She couldn't speak, her body shaking, her sex throbbing. All she could do was nod.

He reared and, hauling her to the edge of the side table, lifted her into his solid thrust, penetrating a fraction farther.

Her sob of bliss mingled with his grunt. He began to move, fast and hard. His powerful plunges should have hurt, but instead his thick hard shaft sent her into delirium, his strokes so deep they drove her wild.

"I love how tightly you're clasping my cock."

She had no response. She was beyond words and burning with fever for this man. His palm was pressed to the wall, his free hand to the small of her back holding her in place as he drove his cock into her with bedeviling skill. Gabrielle simply held on, his mouth tantalizing that sensitive spot below her ear, her neck, her shoulder. She was overwhelmed with sensations.

"You're on the edge, Silvie," he rasped in her ear. "You're about to come for me, aren't you? I can feel your sweet little clenches."

Dear God. She couldn't control that either. Tiny contractions were rippling through her core, around his ramming cock. The physical reactions he could elicit from her body astounded her. Physical reactions she'd no idea how to curb or quell. Her release was imminent. She could feel it coming on. Fast. Sensed it was going to be shattering, and that immediately frightened her. He frightened her. His power over her was so intense. So strong. She was terrified to be that vulnerable to him. She'd struggled against men who wielded power over her all entire life.

Wavering on the edge of orgasm, Gabrielle fought it back. Afraid to let go.

He had her mouth, possessing it with his tongue, his taste intoxicating. His thrusts, sublime. "Let go, Silvie," he murmured. "Don't fight it, *chère*. Give yourself over to the pleasure." But still she fought back her orgasm, violently shaking with effort, her body rioting for release. Trying to outlast him.

"Why don't we give that pretty clit of yours some attention?" she heard him say.

Oh, no . . . Before she could react, he'd pulled his hand from the wall, slipped it between their bodies, and without missing a stroke, he captured the bud between his fingers and pinched it—applying the most perfect pressure.

Her senses exploded with blinding ecstasy. She surged up hard against him, screaming into his mouth. He didn't relent, not with the force of his thrusts or his hold on her pulsating clit, ramming her through the untamable spasms contracting her slick walls. Her body was awash with waves of stunning sensations. Then she felt it—the ripples of another hot wave of rapture. Right on the heels of the first. This time she didn't fight it. This time she let it crash over her, abandoning herself to it, her body shuddering from the force.

Gabrielle willingly let herself drown in the soul-satisfying pleasure flooding through her system. Vaguely, she was aware of his hand slipping out from between their bodies, his fingers gripping her hips and his body stiffening. He reared just then, jerking his cock out and crushed her to him.

Burying his face in her hair, he roared out his pleasure against the curve of her neck, his strong body racked with its own release as his warm semen shot onto her thigh and hip.

She tightened her arms around him, and held him, their labored breaths the only sound in the room.

Dear God, she felt euphoric. She couldn't believe it. *She* actually felt . . . *happy*. It was the first time in a long time.

Mathias's muscles were heavy as lead. His legs weak. He couldn't recall the last time he came that hard. But the wonderful languidness he felt quickly dissipated as questions began to crowd his mind and clear the sexual fog.

Questions he was going to bloody well have answers to.

He forced himself to pull away from her warm soft form and break from her embrace. And his body instantly balked over the loss.

The moment their gazes locked, his heart squeezed tightly. Her cheeks pink, her hair mussed, she looked adorable, sweet, and so damned beautiful—very much like the innocent she was. For the first time since he'd met her, her eyes were truly unguarded. Open and honest.

They told him she was a little shaken, a little wary, out of sorts, and unsure what he was about to do, how he was about to react, now that he knew she'd been a virgin. *Dieu.* Quelling the raw emotions swirling through him, Mathias scooped up the first article of clothing he touched from the pile on the floor, and grabbed the base of his prick, noticing the telltale signs of her lost innocence in the red streaks on it. She looked away, her eyes downcast, her blush deepening the coloring on her cheeks.

He wiped himself clean, then quickly wiped off her soft thigh and silky hip. Crumpling the caleçons in his hand, he tossed them away and slipped his hand under her chin, capturing her undivided attention.

"We're going to talk."

He saw disappointment flash in her dark eyes. *Jésus-Christ.* Did she think he was simply going to let this go? He'd just taken her virginity. He'd thought she was sexually experienced. She was supposed to be Gaillard's mistress.

He never would have said the things he'd said to her, done the things he'd done, had he known she'd been a virgin.

He felt his ire mounting just thinking about the entire mess, a million questions spinning in his head. The more he learned about this woman, the less he knew.

"Would it be all right if I used the *salle de bain* to . . . wash up a little first?" Her voice was soft. Gone was that hard edge she usually had. And the wall that was always up—the one she hid behind—was conspicuously missing.

Merde. You just took her innocence. At least let her refresh herself before you make demands of her. Curbing his anger, his frustration, his impatience, he helped her down off the side table.

"Of course," he said.

She thanked him. Sliding out from between him and the table, she bent and picked up her chemise. He watched her raise her arms and slip it on, admiring her lush curves, her pretty breasts—not too big or small—and then there were those gorgeous legs. God, how he loved women's legs, and hers went on forever. He could still feel their silky strength wrapped around his hips.

As she left the room, he was sure of one thing. She was never Gaillard's mistress. The man would have bedded her before setting her up in his townhouse, providing her with a full staff.

Mathias braced his hands on the edge of the side table and blew out a breath. Damn it. What was going on here?

You didn't want things to get more involved. Well, things just got a hell of a lot more complicated.

A virgin.

He took a *virgin*.

Of all the different kinds of women he'd bedded, this was a bloody first.

He shoved himself away from the table and began to pace. He was livid with himself. He'd noticed signs of her inexperience. In her kiss, in the way she touched him. In the look on her face when he'd played with her clit. As if it were novel. A decadent new discovery. The wonder and delight in her eyes alone were telling.

And he'd ignored every sign. Purposely closing a blind eye just so that he could sink his cock in her.

From the beginning she hadn't wanted to tell him a thing about herself. She hadn't wanted to confide in him a single truth.

And it bothered him more than he could ever say.

He'd just had sex with a woman he didn't know a thing about, and it was torturing him. He was no stranger to anonymous sexual encounters. He'd no idea why he should give her secrecy a second thought. She didn't seem bothered that he'd just claimed her virginity. Why should he be?

Lord knows he had enough to deal with.

Navers and his mission for the Lieutenant General of Police were where his focus should be. Not on this one woman who was at every turn up to no good.

Mathias stopped pacing, raked a hand through his hair, and let out a sharp breath. He walked over to the wash basin in the room, poured water into the bowl, and sluiced it onto his face. He washed, wishing that he could purge her from his thoughts by simply washing her wonderful scent from his skin.

He couldn't let this rest. He simply had to know who she was. What she was all about. And he was finding out as soon as his little secretive seductress reentered the room.

CHAPTER SIX

The moment she reentered the room, her dark eyes swept the bedchamber, surprise flashing in their depths when she spotted him lying casually on his side, naked in her bed.

Propped up on his elbow, Mathias patted the spot beside him. "Come here," he beckoned.

He saw her take a deep breath and let it out slowly before she complied and slipped in bed beside him.

Rolling onto her side, she mimicked his pose, and Mathias could tell that while she'd been in the other room, she'd managed to erect her usual wall.

The barrier was firmly in place between them, solid and true.

And he was going to knock the fucking thing down.

"Take off your chemise," he said. An easier barrier to remove between them.

That took her off balance. By her expression, it was obvious that wasn't what she expected him to say. "Pardon?"

"You don't need it." His tone was gentle yet firm. As was his gaze.

She hesitated for a moment, then sat up, pulled the article off, and tossed it onto the floor. She returned to her pose on her side, looking a little more self-conscious than before.

Her bravado was a little askew. He hoped that would work in his favor.

"You owe me some honest answers, given what just occurred. Let's begin with something simple. What's your name?" he asked, trying to ignore her many female attributes, especially those pretty nipples, trying not to think about how good they'd tasted on his tongue.

"Silvie."

"Your full name."

"What difference does that make?"

He tilted her chin up a notch. "The difference is I just claimed your innocence. Now answer me."

"And do you know the name of every woman you tumble?"

"No, but I think it's a good idea I learn the identity of all those who pretend to be a nobleman's mistress, but turn out to be a virgin."

"I didn't say I was Gaillard's mistress. It's something you assumed."

"And you did nothing to acquit me of the notion. Now let's start again. What is your name?" His voice was a bit louder, sharper. *Merde*. Why was this question so difficult?

"I'm not going to answer that," she stated.

He clenched his jaw, holding back the expletives bellowing in his head. This woman was beyond maddening. "Why the hell not? Is it because you can't or you won't."

"Both."

"Who is Gaillard to you?"

She bit her lip, clearly considering whether or not to answer. Finally she said, "He's a member of my family."

Wonderful. The man's family was huge. It was going to take considerable effort, not to mention time, to eliminate them one by one until he figured out the identity of this particular woman.

A weary sigh escaped her. "Mathias." She placed a hand on his chest. His unruly cock immediately jerked in response. "If you are worried you are going to be dragged to the altar because of what happened tonight, rest easy. That isn't going to happen. No one is going to force you to marry me. I am not seeking a husband . . . although . . ."

He removed her hand from his chest, her touch a serious distraction. "Although?" he prompted.

She lowered her eyes. "One is being selected for me by my father."

He'd no idea why her words felt like a blow to the belly. He felt . . . winded. "Do you know who your husband will be?" Why in the world did he ask that? Why on earth would he care to know?

"No."

Just talking about her getting married was tightening his vitals. He changed the subject. "Why are you here? Why aren't you at home? Why are you playing Basset? Is this some sort of thrill or are you doing it because you have to?"

"Because I have to."

"To cover a debt? You're trying to win back money?"

"Yes."

"Your debt?"

She shook her head. "No, someone else's."

"*Merde*. If your father is looking for a husband for you, there must be some sort of dowry. Your father has means." Someone prominent if she was part of Gaillard's family. Thus the need for her to hide her identity with a disguise. "Get him to pay the debt and stop going to Navers's gaming den."

"I can't ask my father to help. He'd never do it. I've got to do this myself. On my own. And I can't lose the diamonds either." She suddenly looked tired. Lowering her head onto the pillow, she tucked her hands under her cheek. "Not a single diamond."

He brushed an errant curl off her cheek. "Why?"

"Because I took them from him, and he doesn't know."

Jésus-Christ. "Who is it you're helping?"

"Another family member."

"Why not get Gaillard to help you?"

"Because he doesn't know about it and he wouldn't help if he did. No one in the family will help—not to clear a gambling debt. Just me. I had to trick Gaillard just to let me stay here."

"Where does your father think you are?"

"A sojourn . . . with Gaillard at his country estate. I have to return home next week. I have until then to win back the money to cover the debt."

That left only two more nights of Basset before she'd have to leave. He admired her loyalty. Her strength. He didn't know any woman who would have had the courage to do what she'd done.

And he knew, behind that hardened exterior, she was scared.

Mathias caressed her soft cheek with the back of his fingers. "Why don't you let me give you the money and we can put an end to the Basset games."

At that, she jerked her head up off the pillow and frowned. "No. I do things on my own. I won't be beholden. Not to anyone. I can do this—by myself."

He shook his head and muttered a curse. "Silvie, it's a game of chance. There are no guarantees."

"I *can* do this," she repeated a little stronger. "And I will do it, by next week." She rolled onto her other side, once again tucking her hands under her cheek, her delicate back now facing him.

"You know," he said, placing a hand on her shoulder, "you can lean on people for help when you need it. You can trust people."

"No, you can't. You can't trust anyone."

Mathias realized then the magnitude of her gift to him tonight. She'd never trusted anyone, yet she'd trusted him. She'd surrendered herself to him, and it hadn't been easy for her. In the throes of passion, he'd noted how she'd struggled with it.

She gave you a gift she could only give one man. And she picked you. That notion wound around his heart.

He reached out and tucked her up against his body, pleased she didn't pull away. He was hard, but he wasn't going to make any sexual advances. Taking a woman's virginity on a side table was bad enough, but he'd done something he'd never done before during sex.

He'd lost control.

The way he'd ridden her had been too aggressive for an innocent. His conduct shocked him. His actions were always controlled and measured in any sexual encounter. The motions too well practiced for anyone, much less a sexual novice, to unravel him.

Mathias dipped his head, bringing his mouth near her ear. "You're making it easy for me to learn who you are, Silvie. A few well-put questions to Gaillard and I will know your name."

She shrugged with a gentle rise and fall of her shoulder. "I doubt he'll be forthcoming, but if he is, it doesn't matter. By the time you learn anything, I will be home and married off."

Again that tightness gripped him, only this time it squeezed around his heart.

"And what are you going to do about your lack of innocence?" he asked. "Your future husband will expect a virgin bride."

"That's what he'll get. I have half sisters who have managed to fool their husbands on their wedding night into believing their maidenhead was still intact. I'll do the same."

His brows shot up. "You're going to *trick* him?"

She turned and met his gaze over her shoulder. "What difference does it make if I'm not a virgin on the night of the wedding? All he's after is an heir. As long I provide him with a legitimate heir, the rest isn't any of his concern. And the child will be his. That much I'll do. Then he'll leave me alone, and I won't matter beyond that—which suits me just fine."

He couldn't help but wonder what had hardened her so. She wasn't as detached as she wanted the world to believe. Clearly, she had tremendous compassion. She was going to great lengths to help someone in her family. Someone she loved a great deal. Whom others refused to aid. "I don't believe you, Silvie. You make it sound as though you want very little in life."

"What more is there for a woman to want? A marriage to a highborn noble. Children." Her tone was flat, just as before. He got the distinct impression that at some point in her life, she'd stopped wishing for things altogether.

"And what matters to you?" he asked. "Surely, there's got to be something you want."

There was a lengthy silence, and for a moment, Mathias thought she wasn't going to answer.

She rested her head back down onto the pillow and tucked her hands beneath her cheek once more. "I want to leave my father's home. I don't like it there," she said at last.

His brow furrowed with concern. "Have they hurt you?"

She didn't turn around, but this time there was no hesitation with her response. "Don't be ridiculous. No one hurts me. I don't let them."

*****

"Dear Lord, this only gets worse!" Bernadette fretted.

"*Shhhh!* Keep your voice down." Gabrielle frowned and glanced at the closed double doors to her bedchamber. Mathias was asleep inside and voices easily carried through from the antechamber of her private apartments.

As ladies-in-waiting, it was her friends' duty to help her dress each day. It was considered an honor to be that close to a member of the royal family, and thus, the positions were given only to women born into the nobility. Bernadette and Caroline had arrived mere moments before. Upon hearing their voices in her antechamber, Gabrielle awoke, threw on her chemise, and dashed out of her room before they could walk in to find Mathias in her bed.

She'd been forced to tell them he was here.

They surmised the rest.

Caroline was pacing in front of the hearth, wringing her hands, wearing out a path in the wooden floor. "First you steal some royal gems, then you lie about your whereabouts. Now you've . . . you've . . ."

"Been bedded," Gabrielle supplied calmly.

Caroline stopped dead in her tracks. "Yes . . . *bedded*. You're no longer a virgin, and you're to be married."

Bernadette slapped her palms against her cheeks and shook her head. "If the King finds out any of this," she said in a loud whisper, "I don't want to think about what he'll do. To all of us!"

Gabrielle marched over to her friends and, grasping each by an arm, dragged them over to the farthest corner from her bedchamber door. "You'll not mention the King again," she said, *sotto voce*, then paused to cast a glance at her bedchamber door and listened, thankful of the silence. "You'll call me Silvie. Nothing else. Mathias knows nothing about who I am, and I intend to keep it that way. You'll do nothing—absolutely nothing—to give me away. Understood?"

They nodded.

"You said he is the Marquis de Montfort. He's a man of means, no? Couldn't he advance you some funds to cover your brother's debt?" Caroline asked, hopeful. "He clearly likes you."

"That's an excellent idea!" Bernadette smiled. "Then we can return home with the diamonds and all will be well, as if we'd never left . . . except for the part about a missing maidenhead."

Gabrielle let out an exasperated sigh. "It is not an excellent idea. It is a bad one."

Caroline nodded glum. "I suppose it would be rather inappropriate to ask the man bedding you for funds. It would be as though he's paying for . . . well, you know." She blushed.

Gabrielle released her hold on their arms. "I don't have to ask him. He's already offered to pay Daniel's debt, and I turned him down."

Bernadette's mouth fell agape. She clamped it shut. "You told him about Daniel?"

"Never mind that!" Caroline waved her hand. *"You turned him down?"*

She had. And she'd been struggling with the soft sentiment his offer had inspired ever since. Again she found herself comparing Mathias to the men she knew. None of the men at court would have offered to help her unless there was political gain in it for them. Unless doing so would elevate them in the eyes of the King.

And since Gabrielle wasn't one of His Majesty's favorite daughters, men didn't waste their time and effort on her. All forms of generosity and assistance were for those who had the King's esteem.

She hadn't expected Mathias to offer to help.

Not since her mother had anyone extended a hand to her for no other reason than to aid her. She'd stopped expecting people to help her a long time ago.

He'd unbalanced her in the worst way with his offer and his return of her diamonds—for which she was deeply grateful. And though it would be easier to believe the worst of him, her instincts told her he was sincere. That these weren't merely ploys to gain her trust.

She believed him, despite her comments about not trusting anyone. It was an unprecedented first. Utterly uncharacteristic and astonishing, actually.

She wouldn't accept his touching offer or divulge her identity, but she couldn't deny how moved she was by him.

"I'll not be beholden to him. Or anyone." At least not more than she already was. She had to force the words off her tongue.

Words that normally came second nature to her.

The urge to lean on him—when she'd always stood strongly on her own—was fierce. And unsettling. She couldn't allow Mathias to affect her any more than he already had. Her future, though glum and beyond her control, led away from him. She could never permit herself to forget that. Or to leave her heart exposed for him to enter it.

Once she returned home next week, she wanted no ties with him. No attachment of any kind. She'd decided this morning she'd continue a physical involvement with him, but only until she returned to the palace.

That was as far as she was willing to go.

"I don't need his money," she continued. "I am going to win what I need. I have a good feeling my luck has changed." Gabrielle glanced at Bernadette. "As for Daniel, Mathias doesn't know the particulars. He's simply aware I'm playing to win enough funds to cover a debt for a member of my family."

Just then she heard stirrings from inside her bedchamber.

"You must go." She pushed them toward the door but they didn't make it in time. Mathias opened the door to the bedchamber.

Her head snapped in his direction, her breath lodging in her throat at the sight that greeted her.

On the threshold of her antechamber, with nothing more than a sheet of fine bed linen around his hips, Mathias stood—in all his muscled glory.

"*Oh my . . .*" Bernadette breathed. Then whispered, "Will you look at those arms? Solid and hard like sculpted marble . . . and then there's the rest of him . . . I completely understand why you are sans a maidenhead today."

Caroline slapped Bernadette's arm. "Bernadette!" she whispered sharply.

Gabrielle ignored their comments, too captivated by the masculine beauty before her, her blood already heating for him without so much as a touch, her mind conjuring hot memories of those strong arms around her, that muscled body against her, and heaven help her, that delicious part of his male anatomy stroking inside her sheath.

"He's far more than merely beautiful to behold and carnally gifted, and you well know it . . ." a voice whispered deep inside. She muted it immediately.

"Good morning, ladies," he said, his voice rich and inflaming, his light-colored eyes sweeping past Bernadette and Caroline before they locked on to her. A tiny shiver quivered through her.

Gabrielle cleared her throat as her friends returned his greeting. "Good morning, Mathias. My friends"—she gestured behind her—"were leaving. Weren't you?" she said to the two women standing in a trance beside her, openly gawking at the man. Gabrielle elbowed Bernadette, simply because she was the closest.

Bernadette jumped. "Hmm? Oh, yes. We were just leaving. Come, Caroline."

"Oh . . . Yes, of course." Caroline smiled politely.

Both women bade him good day and proceeded to the door when Bernadette abruptly stopped, turned, and out of habit, despite Gabrielle's order not to curtsy to her during their stay at her uncle's townhouse, she began to sink low. Gabrielle rushed forward, threw an arm around her shoulders.

"Oh, Bernadette, don't tell me your knee is acting up again?" Gabrielle said, giving her a stern look, one that silently reprimanded for her blunder.

It took a moment for understanding to appear in Bernadette's eyes. "Ah yes, my *knee* . . ." She glanced at Mathias. "My knee acts up every so often, you see." Bernadette bent forward and rubbed it through her gown.

A rather poor performance. The woman was definitely not meant for the stage.

Gabrielle noted Mathias's frown but, to her relief, saw no sign of suspicion. "Caroline, why don't you take Bernadette to her rooms."

Caroline moved forward and supported Bernadette as she pretended to limp.

"Do you need assistance?" Mathias asked.

"No. Please don't worry." Gabrielle answered for her with a smile, once again touched by his kindness. "She's fine. She has Caroline. Isn't that so, Bernadette?"

"Yes, I'm quite capable of returning on my own . . . with Caroline's help, that is," Bernadette quickly added.

A slight smile lifted the corner of his mouth. "All right then." He moved his gaze to Gabrielle. "I'll wait for you inside," he said, setting her pulse racing with heated excitement. With that, he reentered her bedchamber, closing the door behind him.

She turned to her friends who'd once again slipped into a trancelike state and were still staring at the spot where Mathias had been standing. Gabrielle's smile grew, her insides danced wildly. She couldn't wait to join him.

"I've decided to keep him for a few days. Please be careful around him." She couldn't muster a stern tone, not when she felt so light.

Not when pure bliss was waiting for her on her bed.

Gabrielle walked out of the antechamber and into her bedchamber. Sure enough, lying across the width of her bed was solid male allure.

Perhaps it was because she'd finally had some sleep last night, the first time since she'd arrived in Paris. Or perhaps it was because of the Marquis on her bed who'd brought her more joy in one eve than she'd had in years, but she couldn't remove the smile from her face.

She stopped at the end of her bed.

Propped up on his elbow, Mathias returned her smile.

Dieu, she had a beautiful smile. It lit up her face and caused the most adorable dimples to form on either side of her luscious mouth. He held out a hand, pleased by how quickly she stepped forward and took it.

He brought her hand to his mouth and pressed a soft kiss to her knuckle. "Take off your chemise." He felt a tremor of excitement quiver through her, and that pleased him further still. Beneath the bed linen wrapped around his waist, he was at a full cock-stand. In fact, he was hard from the moment he laid eyes on her in the antechamber in that knee-length undergarment.

He watched as she slid the hem up her thighs, her belly, to finally sweep it up over her erect nipples and off, the linen garment falling to the floor.

Soft curves and satiny skin, she looked so good. With her standing this close to him, he could detect the soft scent of her arousal, an aphrodisiac to his senses, his every muscle tightening with hunger.

"You are a vision." He never meant anything more sincerely.

It was easy to forget she'd been an innocent last eve—that is, until he noticed her averted gaze, and the pretty blush coloring her cheeks.

She wasn't quite used to being naked before him. He didn't want her being embarrassed or inhibited around him in any way. He wanted her unrestrained. Unabashed. Without hesitation of any kind.

And without the wall she erected between them. Last night had been a start. A very good start. She'd entrusted him with some details about herself, and he knew that wasn't easy for her.

More than anything, he wanted her to learn to open up to him. In and out of bed.

And when it came to the boudoir, he was going to make certain she never held back from him again—the way she'd attempted to last eve in the throes of passion.

And there was no time like the present to begin working on that.

Mathias sat up.

He took her hand and pulled, bending her forward for a kiss, his fingers threading in her hair as he savored her taste. She softly moaned against his mouth. Normally, he wouldn't still be in a woman's bed in the morning. He'd made it a habit to leave after sex. Staying any longer, in his experience, gave the mistaken impression that the amorous encounter was something more than just recreational.

Yet he couldn't bring himself to leave her sleeping form last night.

He was so inexplicably drawn to this woman, it was mind-bending.

"Come here," he said giving her arm a sharp pull, purposely making her lose her balance. She fell across his lap with a surprised yelp, her hips resting on his linen-covered thighs.

Rising up onto her elbows, she tossed him a questioning look over her shoulder. "Mathias, what are you doing?"

"It isn't fair to pay tribute to just the front part of your delectable body, *chère*. I think equal adoration should be given to your backside, especially . . ." He ran a light hand over her luscious bottom, making her squirm. "When you have such a beautiful derrière."

He caressed her bottom once more, luxuriating over its sweet curve and delighting in the feel of her skin. She gave him a little wiggle.

"Mathias . . ." There was a tinge of breathlessness to her tone. Planting her palms onto the mattress, she started to rise. Gently, he pressed her down onto the bed with a firm hand against her back. She was deliciously draped over his lap, inspiring a number of salacious ideas, and he wasn't anywhere close to being done.

"Not yet, Silvie. Just relax. I'm not going to hurt you."

She looked unsure, almost leery about what his intentions were while he had her across his lap, but she didn't protest further and she didn't try to rise.

That she was putting trust in him at the moment made him happier than he'd ever admit.

He slipped his hands between her thighs and spread her legs apart, feeling her stiffen, a mixture of innocent apprehension and arousal. The way her body was angled, her bottom tilting up, he had a perfect view of her glistening pink softness. She had the prettiest sex he'd ever seen. Lovely nether lips. And the sweetest little clit. A man could spend hours with his head buried between these long silky thighs in oral worship.

At the first stroke of his fingers over her sleek folds, she lost her breath.

"You're wet for me." He smiled at her deepening blush, and tenderly massaged her soaked sex. She was resting on her forearms, her head turned and her dark eyes watching him. Already her breaths were becoming choppy and quick. Closely watching her reactions, he kept the pressure of his strokes consistent, gliding his slick fingers over her clit from time to time, purposely giving her little jolts of heightened sensation to build her hunger, keep her keen.

"You like this, Silvie?" He brushed her clit again, enjoying her soft cry.

"Yes . . ." She panted and pushed up against his hand, trying to rub her engorged little bud against his evasive fingers. "I want . . . *oh!* . . . I . . . want . . ."

He loved how she was becoming less coherent, more feverish. His strong, spirited Silvie was unraveling, and watching it happen before his eyes hardened his cock to painful proportions.

"What do you want?" He was stroking the slit of her sex, milking more heated responses. He liked the sound of her moans, her occasional little wiggle and lifting of her bottom.

"I . . . I want . . . you . . . inside me."

"As you wish." He thrust two fingers into her tight warm core.

She let out a mixture of a cry and a sob, her hips jerking hard. Holding her firmly, he immediately went to work on that sweet hot spot inside her feminine walls, giving it short quick strokes that made her buck, her legs shake. She whimpered and tried to squirm away. Knowing the sensations over that ultrasensitive gland were deliciously intense, Mathias tightened his hold, keeping her in place, letting her get used to the erotic sensation, without playing with her clit, all the while plying her with steady strokes.

His name rushed past her lips on a pant. She was wiggling harder, unable to hold still. He soothed her with words, coaxed her along, encouraging her to give herself over to the pleasure, telling her how good she felt around his fingers, how hard a release he was going to give her.

Within moments, she was widening her legs, giving him easier access, and rocking her hips with mouthwatering allure. She'd dropped her chin, her hair hiding her face, her trembling now stronger than before. Her sex soaked his busy fingers with more juices.

Jésus-Christ. She was on the edge. And so was he. "You're going to come for me, without holding back in any way." It wasn't a question.

"Y-Yes!" She confirmed what he could feel around his fingers. If he wasn't so hard, his cock so unbearably full, he might have smiled. No hesitation there. Just sweet surrender.

Her orgasm hit her hard, wrenching a scream from her. She stiffened.

With lightning movements, Mathias pulled his hand out of her contracting sheath, yanked off the sheet around his waist, and stuffed a pillow under her hips to keep her bottom angled.

He filled her quivering core with one fluid stroke, pushing his whole length into her, knowing she liked it deep. She mewed a welcome, followed by a shiver of delight, accepting his possession, taking his deep long thrusts, her slick walls decadently pulsing around him.

He basked in those wild uncontrollable clenches, holding back his climax, shaking with the effort. Her body sucking him in with each glorious spasm, she was hot and soft and exquisitely snug; she had the most incredible cunt he'd ever known.

Just as her contractions began to ebb, his control snapped. Ecstasy slammed into him. He pulled out, his semen purging from his prick with stunning force, pouring himself onto her sweet bottom, until he was completely drained dry.

Collapsing onto his back beside her, he was as boneless as she. It took him several moments before he could calm his breathing and move his muscles. Grabbing her chemise, he cleaned them both, tossed the thing to the floor, and gently eased the pillow from under her hips.

Her breathing almost normal, she rolled onto her side facing him, her hands tucked under her cheek. Propped up on his elbow, he gazed into her eyes, noting the soft look—the very same softness he'd seen in her eyes last eve. They lay there in silence, but it wasn't awkward. In fact, there was a deep serenity to it, the likes of which he'd never experienced before.

He caressed her cheek, allowing himself to enjoy the features of her lovely face. She had no exotic coloring, but she was a classic beauty. And *Dieu*, he loved her height. She fit perfectly with his body, as though she were made just for him.

In the quiet of the moment, he didn't sense a wall between them, that barrier she kept between her and the rest of the world. The look in her eyes was far from detached and he fully expected her to erect a barrier posthaste.

Taking advantage of her amenable state, he said, "You can trust me with your secrets, just as you've trusted me with your body. I won't hurt you, Silvie. I won't betray your confidence or turn your secrets against you." He cradled her cheek in his palm. She lowered her gaze. Mathias placed a soft kiss on her lips, wishing he knew her thoughts. Wishing he knew how to silence this incessant desire to know more about her. "Tell me something, anything about yourself. Something I don't already know."

She lifted her gaze to his. "I've never met anyone like you," she responded with as much sincerity in her eyes as in her tone.

He was taken aback by the endearing comment.

Tenderly, he stroked his thumb across her cheek. "Tell me something you've never told anyone else."

She put her arms around him, snuggled up against him. "I'm glad I met you," she whispered in his ear. "That's something I've never told anyone else."

Her words took him by surprise and melted his heart.

He pulled her tightly against him, his arms acting on their own volition, returning her embrace, unable to dispel the notion that this was so right. Unable to mute the tender emotions welling inside him. Emotions he had no desire to halt from happening.

Merde. The last woman he should involve himself with was one with as many secrets as Silvie had.

Gabrielle closed her eyes, relishing the simple pleasure of being in the circle of his strong arms. She felt safe and, God help her, protected. She swallowed hard against the lump in her throat. The temptation to reveal all to him was so great.

She couldn't.

She was going to hold on to this last level of detachment. This final bit of distance. Why open herself up totally? She'd have to leave him soon and it would only hurt more if she did. It was clear the longer she spent with him, the more she fell under his spell. She'd already opened herself up to him in ways she'd never had with anyone else.

There were a thousand reasons why she should end this now. Why she should send him home. And only one reason why he should remain.

Contentment.

Near him, she felt content. It was novel. It was wonderful. And oh so irresistible.

Married or not, there were many more empty years ahead of her. Did she have the strength to deny herself more of this man?

Lifting her head, she met his beautiful gray eyes, and then the words she'd been grappling with tumbled from her lips. "Will you stay?"

CHAPTER SEVEN

"Ten wins. Six loses."

Mathias couldn't believe it. She had won another *sept-et-le-va*. How fortunate could one person be in a game that was mathematically stacked against the player, in favor of the banker?

Her winnings tonight had more than covered the losses from the last game.

Though he knew she was pleased, she did an excellent job schooling her features. Not acting exuberant in any way. No one who gambled at Basset celebrated each win.

Not when luck was a fickle mistress. At times she loved you. More often, she left you.

Especially in Basset.

The more he played, the more he fucking hated this game. Far too many tragedies were occurring because of it. Not an hour ago, another prominent family had come to ruin. At the table next to him, the Baron de Tremblay had lost his entire fortune. Mathias's entrails twisted in his gut watching the man leave Navers's drawing room sobbing. And he wasn't the only one affected. Silvie was just as grief-stricken for Tremblay. He'd seen it flash in her eyes before she masked the emotion.

Tonight, Mathias wasn't experiencing any of Silvie's good fortune. He couldn't concentrate. Not just because of Tremblay's loss. It was Valette. The police sergeant's eyes had been on him the entire night. Valette was at the next table over and he could actually feel the weasel's stare.

Casting a glance in Valette's direction, he locked eyes with the man.

Mathias looked back at his cards, fighting the urge to gnash his teeth.

Something wasn't right. Ever since yesterday when Valette had paid him another visit, he couldn't shake his feeling of unease. Valette told him that Sard wanted more names.

Twenty players were in attendance tonight—same as the last time. So far, he'd managed to decipher the identities of a total of seventeen of them.

But there was something else going on. He had a gnawing feeling that something was going to happen. Something was being hatched by Sard and his sergeant that Mathias wasn't privy to. In the pit of his belly, he feared there might be a raid on the Duc's home.

Every time the door opened, he lost his focus and tensed.

Valette had said he wanted the names of *all* in attendance. He kept insisting that everyone had to be held accountable. That it was important that the arrests would be numerous.

But there was one name he couldn't give.

Mathias pulled his gaze to Silvie. Even if he knew her name, he'd never tell Sard or Valette. Short of telling her about his mission, he'd done his damnedest over the last few days to convince her to stay away from Navers's gaming table.

To no avail.

She'd donned her male attire and here she was, winning a small fortune, just as she'd predicted. *Merde*, her breasts were bound, her head covered with that ridiculous periwig, and her feminine form completely concealed, and he was hard just looking at her, knowing under all that was Silvie.

His Silvie.

He'd spent the last four glorious days with his beautiful Snow Princess sitting in the courtyard of her townhouse, under the sun's warm rays, listening to her read him her favorite poems. He'd developed an appreciation for poetry he'd never had before. Poetry didn't mix with his previous life of vice.

And then there were the magnificent nights sharing carnal delights with her. He only pulled himself away from her a few hours a day to change his clothes and attend to matters at home.

There was no finer bliss than time with this complex, fascinating woman. But their time was running out.

There were only a few days more until the next Basset game at Navers's home. Then she'd be gone. He tried his hardest to ignore the ache that thought left in his chest. It was even harder to push away gut-wrenching thoughts of her married to another man. And his claiming his conjugal rights.

This wasn't at all his normal reaction to the imminent end of an affair.

Every day that brought him closer to the date of her departure increased his emotional turmoil. He was riddled with soft emotions for a woman who was still a mystery, his ceaseless desire to know everything about her adding to his inner torment. As was his mission—one he couldn't tell her a damned thing about.

And he hated, loathed all the secrets between them.

"Queen wins. Seven loses."

His body went rigid. *Merde.* She'd just lost her wager. A tidy sum.

Silvie rose, surprising him. "I've had enough," she announced, and scooped up her winnings. Mathias couldn't have been more relieved to see her go. The sooner she got out of here, the better. At least she'd heeded his advice about leaving the table once her luck had turned. She was still walking out with a sizable win.

Navers rose. "Why leave so soon? Stay for another game."

Never one to be told what to do, his Snow Princess remarked, "I'll see you at the next game." Then she walked around the Duc and left the room.

Mathias wanted nothing more than to leave with her, but Valette was watching and he decided he'd play another hour.

*****

Gabrielle tucked her pouch of diamonds and winnings back under her mattress.

She wasn't sleeping much at night. Mathias and his delicious kisses and decadent lovemaking were the new cause for her sleeplessness.

But she didn't mind. She gloried in it, grateful for knowing him, for having created memories to cherish.

Removing her periwig, she let down her hair and sat on the edge of her bed in her men's attire. The hour was late and she wasn't going to bother changing.

Mathias would be leaving the gaming den and arriving soon. Before he intoxicated her with his touch, she was going to have a talk with him.

The devastating loss by one of the players tonight had shaken her. Just as it had the last time.

Seeing the abject horror in Mathias's eyes as the man left sobbing had astounded her.

The reaction seemed out of place—too strong for a seasoned gambler like Mathias. He had to have seen losses of that magnitude before. More often than she had. Yet, he'd looked utterly stricken.

Equally baffling was the way he kept looking around, as though he was expecting someone.

Footsteps in the corridor yanked her from her thoughts. She rose in anticipation. Within moments Mathias walked into her bedchamber. He smiled when he saw her.

A smile that didn't reach his eyes.

"Congratulations on your win," he said, taking off his justacorps and tossing it on a nearby chair. "You're thrilled, no doubt." He started on the buttons on his vest.

Her insides danced as she watched him undress.

"Yes. I am thrilled. Mathias, there is something I'd like to know."

He tossed off the vest and raked a hand through his dark hair. "Do you have any brandy?" he asked, completely ignoring her statement.

She frowned, but walked over to a wooden cabinet in her bedchamber and opened the doors. Her uncle had a crystal decanter filled with his favorite brandy and crystal glasses there.

The moment Mathias saw the decanter, he marched over. "Allow me," he said.

She stepped away and watched him pour himself an ample amount and drain the crystal vessel just as quickly. To her astonishment, she saw the tremor in his hand as he lifted a fresh goblet to his lips.

"Mathias." She stepped forward, took the goblet from his grip, and set it back down in the cabinet. "What is amiss?"

It was his turn to frown. "What are you talking about?" He walked away undoing his cravat.

"You are in distress. It's rather obvious. What's wrong?"

"Nothing." He tossed the cravat onto the chair and held out a hand. "Come here." She knew that tone. It was carnal in nature. The moment she took his hand, he'd pull her close, kiss her, and scramble her senses.

"No. We need to talk."

"*Merde*, Silvie. The last thing I feel like doing tonight is talking."

"Mathias, why won't you answer me? Why won't you tell me why you are so upset?"

"*Jésus-Christ!*" The words exploded from his mouth, making her jump. "Woman, do you jest? You are actually making demands of me when you won't answer the most basic question?" He was all but hollering at her.

She'd never seen him like this and she refused to let this escalate into a heated argument by raising her tone in return. Not when he was so overwrought. "I am simply concerned about you," she responded softly.

It was clear her gentle voice had impact. He let out a sharp sigh and placed his hands on his hips. "Silvie, I don't want to argue with you, *chère*. *Dieu*, I just plain want you. I just want to hold you and make love to you and forget about everything, including your imminent departure."

At the mention of her leaving, her heart constricted painfully. She walked up to him, laced her arms around his neck, and buried her face in his shoulder. His strong arms encircled her, holding her tightly. Tears stung her eyes and threatened to spill. She blinked them back and composed herself.

The moment she met his gaze, he cupped her face and lowered his mouth onto hers. His kiss was soft and tender and made her ache. Heart and body.

"I wish I didn't have to go," slipped past her lips when he broke the kiss.

He rested his forehead against hers. "So do I."

Lovingly, she caressed his cheek. "Are you all right?"

"Seeing someone lose everything bothers me," he responded, surprising her.

"It was evident on your face."

"I lost a close friend a few months ago. He took his life after losing all that he owned in a game of Basset."

She cupped his face and gave him a gentle kiss. "I'm so sorry, Mathias. Why do you still play if seeing losses upsets you so?"

At that he pulled away from her. "I just do." His tone was tight.

"Is there something you're not telling me about Navers's gaming den? You were always looking at the door."

He cocked his head slightly. "Did you win enough to cover the debt?"

Changing the subject wasn't a good sign. "No. I had almost enough, but then I lost some."

"Does that mean you'll be returning in a few days to play a final game?"

"Yes."

"Silvie, why don't you let me give you the rest?"

Taking his hands, she pulled him toward the bed. Her mind and heart were in wild conflict and she was afraid to answer questions in such a vulnerable state. "I believe you said something about wanting me?" She stopped when the back of her legs bumped the bed. Releasing his hands, she began to open her breeches.

He had the remainder of his clothing off by the time she had the breeches undone and stripped off. He removed her cravat, then her linen shirt, and finally the binding around her chest. Picking her up, he deposited her gently on the bed and stretched out on top of her.

The hot press of his solid body against her set her blood on fire, made her sex slicken.

He dipped his head and grazed his mouth along her neck, a slow fiery path that ignited her senses. "Who is this woman I kiss?" he whispered in her ear. "The one who gave her innocence to me." He spread her legs with his knees and stroked his cock along her slick folds. A soft moan slipped past her lips. "She's wet for me," he groaned. "She gives herself to me . . . comes for me . . . She's given me such pleasure and yet I may never know who she is . . ."

"Please, Mathias. Don't do this. Not now." She was in extreme emotional tumult.

"Tell me something about you." He brushed his mouth over hers. "Tell me anything. Tell me something you've never told anyone else."

"I'll miss you with all my heart."

*****

"We're going to talk," Mathias said the moment he entered Renault de Sard's study. The Lieutenant General of Police rose from his chair.

"Have a seat." He gestured to one of the two silk damask chairs in front of his desk.

"No, I prefer to stand. I'll get right to the point. I want to know when you intend to make arrests. I've given Valette a number of names."

Sard sighed and sat down. "I'm afraid I can't discuss that with you, Montfort."

"Why not?"

"Because the King decides when the arrests will take place and that information remains between His Majesty and me."

"Look, tell the King you have names. You have details. Make your damn arrests and be done with it."

"If only it were that easy."

Mathias narrowed his eyes and planted his palms down on Sard's desk. "What is going on here? What is it you're planning?"

"What I'm planning is to please the King. That is always my plan. He wants to see his ban enforced. Do what is required of you and give me the names of all the players at Navers's gaming den."

"I've given you all the names I know. The players are masked. There isn't a lot of talking. Those are all the names I can come up with. And since I'm no longer of any use to you or the King, I'm done." Mathias pushed himself off the desk.

The corner of Sard's mouth lifted, stopping short of a smile. "You don't get to decide when you're done. His Majesty decides. He's been made aware of your involvement. If this matter takes much longer, he will get impatient. His Majesty wants a *large* arrest."

"Are you planning on a raid on Navers's gaming den?"

"Again, that is none of your concern."

"Damn it! I'm involved here. It is my concern. I did not need to help. I agreed to assist. I have every right to know what the hell is going on."

"Who's the young man?"

Mathias rested his hands on his hips, lest he strangle Sard's thin neck. "What young man?"

"Valette tells me that a young man shows up every time. He sits at your table always and he gambles with diamonds."

Mathias's stomach fisted. "Yes, I know who you mean. I don't know him."

"Really? Valette said he saw you talking to the young man outside near the carriages. He felt you knew him. He said you *touched him*."

Every muscle in his body slowly tightened. *Fuck.* "What the hell are you suggesting, Sard?"

The King's Lieutenant General of Police rose. "Before I approached you, Montfort, I thoroughly investigated you. I felt from what I learned about you, you'd be the perfect man to aid His Majesty and me in this matter. I knew you'd be sympathetic, given the death of your friend. From all accounts, you've not exactly led the life of a saint. Vice was your choice of entertainment. Everything I learned about you suggests you have a penchant for beautiful women."

"So?" His heart was beating in slow hard thuds.

"So if you have secrets, they need to remain that way. I personally selected you and I'll not be embarrassed before the King. Be discreet and I'll not arrest you for your conduct."

"Arrest me for what conduct?"

"Sodomy is a crime."

Mathias reached out across Sard's desk, grabbed his vest, and yanked him forward, their noses all but butting. "I'm going to pretend you didn't say that, Sard."

He'd hardly led a monkish life, but he'd never had any sexual interest in men. As for the law, it was a joke. Everyone in the entire realm knew the King's only brother, Philippe, Duc d'Orléans, preferred men in his bed. The younger the better. It was an open secret no one discussed.

He released Sard. Unfazed, the Lieutenant General held his gaze. "If the young man means nothing to you, get me his name—and conduct yourself in a manner that would please the King. This meeting is over. You are dismissed."

Holding back the profanity burning up his throat, Mathias turned on his heel and stalked out.

Moments later Valette was permitted back into Sard's study.

"Well?" Valette asked.

Sard smoothed his vest and sat back down at his desk. "We're going to go ahead with the raid at the next Basset game Navers hosts in his home."

CHAPTER EIGHT

The afternoon sun was warm and pleasant in the courtyard of Gaillard's townhouse. Seated in the shade of a walnut tree, Gabrielle had a book on her lap. She'd yet to read a single word. Her mind crowded with thoughts, it was difficult to focus on the sonnets.

She was leaving tonight.

Everything was packed. Right after the Basset game, she'd be on her way to her uncle's château, where members of the King's Guard would find her two days hence to escort her back to the palace.

The last few nights with Mathias had been bittersweet.

She didn't want to leave him. But what choice did she have? She was the King's daughter. A princess trapped in a gilded prison, she had to return to Versailles. Return to her role and accept the husband her father selected for her.

Around Mathias she was a different person than she was at court. With him, it was easy to be light. To laugh. It was difficult to be distant with him when all she wanted was to draw near.

She'd never lacked strength in her life. She'd relied on her strength to make it through all these years. But she didn't possess nearly enough to say good-bye. Not to his beloved face.

For that reason, she hadn't told him she was leaving this eve instead of tomorrow, as he believed.

"There you are." Mathias's voice grabbed her attention.

Joy welled up inside her the moment she saw him walking down cobblestone path toward her. The light breeze caressed his dark hair, and his light gray justacorps not only accentuated his broad shoulders, but was a perfect match with those knee-weakening, beautiful eyes.

Her nerve endings sparked to life.

Smiling, he sat down beside her on the stone bench, slipped a hand onto the nape of her neck, and pulled her close for a kiss. Long and luscious and languorous. It was heaven.

He was heaven. Behind her closed eyes, she felt the sting of tears. In the years to come, would he remember her still and think of her from time to time? Or would she fade in his memory?

"I brought you something," he said, smiling.

His smile was contagious. "Oh?"

Reaching inside his justacorps, Mathias pulled out a pink satin box, a little smaller than his palm.

Surprised, she took it from his hands, placed it on her lap, and lifted the pretty lid.

Her eyes immediately filled with fresh tears. She fought them back.

Inside was a small leather-bound volume with the name SILVIE on the cover. Pulling the small book out of the box, she held it in her hands. She was so moved, she couldn't speak.

"It's a book of poetry. I saw it at the bookseller and had the cover custom made," he explained. "Do you like it?"

She nodded, and put her arms around him, her throat tight with emotion. "I'll cherish it always. I'll think of you each time I read it," she said near his ear.

Grasping her wrists, he removed her arms from around his neck and held her hands. "I've been thinking, Silvie. I'd like to speak to your father."

Her brows shot up. "Speak to *my* father? Why?"

He gently squeezed her hands. "Since he is looking for po-tential husbands for you, I'd like him to consider me."

Her heart lost a beat. Dear God, this was the first time Mathias had ever discussed the future—with her in it. Hope surged inside her. She had to tamp it down. "My father isn't exactly an easy man to speak to. He—He may have made his decision. If that is so, he isn't one to change his mind."

"I can be persuasive, Silvie."

Her mind was spinning. Could it work? Might it actually happen?

Dare she wish for it? No, she wasn't going to wish for it. Her father was unpredictable. With the brood of children His Majesty had sired, he usually gave his daughters in marriage to those he favored at court. Like gifts. The probability of the King being amiable to the idea of marrying her to a man who had a reputation for vice was slim. It mattered little that the King himself was vice-ridden. His Majesty rarely saw the irony in things.

"I have to think . . ." she said. "My father isn't easily dealt with . . ."

"I want to marry you, Silvie."

"Why? You don't know me."

"Yes, I do. I know that beneath that hard exterior is a woman who is tender and kind and beautiful from the inside out. She makes me smile. She makes me happy." He leaned in and nuzzled her neck. "She makes me so damned hard." His warm breath tickled her neck and sent a delightful shiver through her. He lifted his head and looked into her eyes.

"I love you, Silvie."

She grabbed his justacorps and kissed him hard, crushing her mouth to his, afraid those same words would slip past her lips. Words she couldn't say. It would shatter her, knowing he couldn't be hers. Knowing her father wouldn't agree. Why pick Mathias when there were scores of men who followed the King around each and every day at the palace whom he knew and liked and wanted to reward?

Mathias's words only weighted her heart more.

He broke the kiss and caressed her cheek. "I have to go. We'll discuss this matter later." He rose. "There is one more thing, Silvie. Under no circumstances are you going to Navers's hôtel tonight. I've left a purse with your majordomo. It is the balance of the debt. You are going to take it and forget Basset. There is going to be trouble, and you're not getting involved in it."

Gabrielle set down the items on her lap on the bench and stood. "What do you mean, 'trouble'?" When he paused she added, "Either you tell me what you mean, or I am going."

He sighed. "Silvie, if I trust you enough to be my wife, and that is what you are going to be regardless, then you need to know there is a chance that there may be a raid tonight by the Paris Police. The King wants his ban on Basset taken seriously."

Gabrielle's pulse began to race. "You're involved? You are helping the Paris Police?"

"Yes, and as committed to it as I am, I'll not hold my tongue about the raid and place you in harm's way."

Her heart began to pound. A most extraordinary plan took shape in her mind. The best one she'd ever devised.

A life-altering plan.

*****

Mathias smiled on his way from Navers's hôtel to Silvie's townhouse. Slumped back in the moving carriage, he felt weary, but happy, and most of all, relieved. It was over.

And he'd been right.

Two hours into the evening, thirty men from the Paris police, including Sard, burst into Navers's home and arrested the Duc, his nephew, and all the players in attendance.

But not Silvie. For once she'd actually heeded his advice. And he was thrilled she wasn't caught. He couldn't wait to see her. To make love to her.

To make plans on broaching her father.

Just how difficult could the man be? Whatever he was like, whoever he was, Mathias would get his way. Silvie would be his. She loved him. He knew it. He knew in time, she'd come to verbally express the emotion that was in her eyes each time she looked at him. Touched him. Kissed him.

The carriage pulled up to the townhouse. He alighted with a bounce in his step. His heart raced, now that he was so close to her.

He couldn't wait to share the details of the night. Describe the look of outrage on the Duc's face. There were enough men of quality there that the sweeping arrest, with a *Lettre de Cachet* for each man Mathias had named, would rock the aristocracy and make them take heed.

The King was deadly serious.

There would be no more Basset.

Mathias stopped before the door to the townhouse. He looked up at the night sky. It was punctured with a million twinkling lights. "Rest in peace, Victor," he said, then knocked on the door.

As usual, the majordomo answered. "Good evening, my lord."

Mathias stepped inside. "Good evening." He proceeded to cross the vestibule. Because he was there every day, he simply showed himself to Silvie's private apartments.

"My lord, the mademoiselle is not here."

Mathias arrested his steps. "What do you mean, not here?" Silvie never left the townhouse, except in disguise to play Basset.

"She left, my lord. She took her party and her trunks and departed this afternoon."

His stomach plummeted. He turned and raced up the stairs, down the hall, and burst into Silvie's rooms. He stopped short in Silvie's bedchamber.

It was empty.

He threw open the doors of the armoires. They were empty, too. He slid his hand beneath her mattress. No diamonds there.

No anything.

Jésus-Christ, she was truly gone! He looked around the empty chamber, incredulous and in shock.

Mathias returned to the vestibule, moving slower down the stairs than he'd ascended them. His legs felt leaden, his insides cold and numb.

The majordomo waited patiently at the bottom.

"Did she leave me a note?" he asked. He hated the desperation in his voice, but at the moment, he didn't care.

"No, my lord."

"A message of some kind with you or perhaps another member of the staff?"

"Any message or note would be given to me, one way or the other. I'm afraid there is nothing, my lord."

"Where did she go?" he demanded, his frustration showing.

"I'm afraid I couldn't say, my lord."

"What is her name? How is she related to your master?"

"My apologies, my lord, but again, I couldn't say."

Wouldn't say was more accurate. But he couldn't blame the servant. Giving out information about one's employer or his houseguest would surely result in the man's dismissal.

Mathias felt as though someone had punched him in the stomach. He couldn't believe she'd left without saying good-bye. Or leaving a note.

He couldn't believe he'd misread her affections. *Fool. You proposed marriage and declared your love.* She neither accepted the former nor claimed the latter. She said she was leaving and she'd left.

Mathias moved to the door. The servant was there promptly to open it for him.

"One last question," Mathias said.

"Of course, my lord."

"The purse I gave you, the coin . . . Did you give that to the mademoiselle?"

"Yes, my lord. I handed it to her personally, just as you requested. She took the purse with her when she left."

Mathias stepped outside, reeling. The door closed softly behind him.

His love was rejected. But apparently his money was acceptable.

CHAPTER NINE

"You know, you should look happier, Montfort," Sard said, stepping down from the carriage after him. "You are at Versailles." He placed a hand on Mathias's shoulder. "Look at it. It's magnificent, beyond opulent. It is a fitting palace for the most powerful monarch in all of Christendom."

Mathias, having shared a carriage with the man from Paris to Versailles, thought nothing could be more annoying than his snoring. He thought wrong. Sard was annoying awake or asleep.

He followed the Lieutenant General of Police into the palace. The servants and guards knew him well and Sard was left to walk through the corridors unchallenged.

"Can you tell me again why the hell we're here?" Mathias asked. He hated court, with all its ludicrous rules. It was hotter than Hades, and yet he was being forced to wear a periwig, as per the King's command that every man of quality wear one at court.

"The King wishes to speak to you. Probably about your assistance with the arrests at Navers's gaming den. We caught nineteen that night. The only one we didn't get was the young man with the diamonds."

At the mention of Silvie, his insides tightened. It had been two weeks since he'd discovered her gone. Thanks to her, agony and anger accompanied him wherever he went. The last thing he felt like doing was having an audience with the King.

They stepped into the Hall of Mirrors, overcrowded with hundreds of courtiers. Curious looks were cast their way as he and Sard walked up the middle of the long corridor. His Majesty was easily spotted. Several carpeted steps higher than the throng before him, he stood in front of his solid silver throne.

Mathias and Sard bowed deeply before him.

"Your Majesty, this is the Marquis de Montfort," Sard said as he and Mathias straightened.

"Your Majesty," Mathias bowed again, unsure what else to do. The King surprised him by climbing down a few steps and stopping before him.

"Sard tells me you were invaluable in the arrests at Navers's home. He has sung your praises, and his own." King Louis gave his Lieutenant General a brief sidelong glance. "He has reminded me on more than a few occasions that he was the one to select you for the mission."

Sard simply smiled.

"I was quite impressed with what you did, Montfort," the King continued. "Sard tells me you didn't require any persuasion and that you were eager to aid in enforcing my ban and worked diligently, demonstrating the utmost commitment to your mission."

Dieu, Sard had really played this up—for his benefit, so *he'd* look good.

"It was an honor to be of assistance, Your Majesty," Mathias said, hoping the audience with the King would end soon. There was no doubt about it; he had an intimidating quality about him. And Mathias was never one to be intimidated easily.

"Your efforts have abounded at the palace, Montfort. You even managed to impress one of my daughters. She thinks quite highly of your character. I find I share her opinion." The

King smiled. "In light of that, I've decided to give you a reward."

"A reward, Your Majesty?"

"Yes, an honor bestowed upon you, by me."

"No reward is necessary, Sire."

"I disagree," the King announced with finality.

Clearly, there would be no debate over it. He was going to keep quiet, take his "reward," and leave. Soon, he hoped.

"I've decided to give you the hand of the very daughter you've impressed so much."

Mathias froze, as did his breathing. There was no way he had heard that correctly.

"You . . . wish me to marry your daughter, Your Majesty?" Praying there was some sort of misunderstanding.

"Yes, you're not married and it is *an honor*," the King stressed again, sounding irked that Mathias was not ecstatic over this madness. *Merde.*

He felt as though he'd stepped into some sort of bad dream. He was being strong-armed into a marriage.

Sard placed a hand on Mathias's shoulder again. "Of course, the Marquis de Montfort knows that, Sire. He's simply overwhelmed by your generosity, aren't you?" Sard squeezed his shoulder.

Mathias cleared his throat. "Yes, this is definitely a surprise, Sire."

King Louis gave a nod. "It is understandable that you are astounded. It isn't every day a man is offered a princess as a bride. I feel your marriage to my daughter would further demonstrate my disdain and intolerance for Basset. I have awarded the man who helped in enforcing the ban one of my own daughters."

Merde.

"I'm sure you're eager to meet your future bride, Montfort." The King glanced about.

About as eager as he would be to sever a limb. He'd been a devoted bachelor. He'd only ever met one woman whom he'd wanted to marry, and she had disappeared.

"Where is Princess Gabrielle?" the King snapped at those around him. Perfect. The man wasn't in one of his more genial moods today.

Mathias simply had to get out of this ludicrous situation. Under no circumstances was he marrying "Princess Gabrielle."

"Here I am, Sire." A too familiar voice snagged his attention.

There was Silvie, elegantly curtsying before the King at the bottom of the steps. Holding her gown, she ascended the steps, and stopped to stand beside her father.

Mathias stood there, mouth agape, barely breathing. *Mother of God, she's a princess . . .*

Sard slapped his arm. He shot him a look. It was then he noticed Sard and the entire throng in the Hall of Mirrors were in a deep curtsy or bow.

Quickly, Mathias bowed before the King's daughter. *Merde.* He'd deflowered the King's daughter. A princess. *Princess Gabrielle.* He'd deflowered a princess. He'd had her numerous times in various ways. He'd thoroughly debauched her.

That's perfect, Mathias. If the King finds out what you did with his daughter, you are a dead man.

"You may rise, sir," she said to him.

He straightened. Her expression schooled, she was standing two steps above him, her hands folded in front of her.

She'd put him through two weeks of hell, thinking she'd not had any affection for him. Clearly, she'd been behind this "reward" of his.

He couldn't be more overjoyed.

Seeing her again, being this close to her made his heart ache. He wanted nothing more than to touch her, pull her into his arms, but the King and his entire court were watching.

"It is a pleasure to meet you, sir." She held out her hand.

Eager, he took it and pressed a kiss to her knuckle. "The pleasure is all mine, Princess." Mathias turned to the King. "Your daughter is beautiful, Sire. I am delighted and honored to have her hand in marriage."

The King gave a nod then descended the steps. "It's too warm in here," he complained and headed to the gardens, the court following behind.

Only when the crowd had moved away, and all but completely dissipated did his princess speak again. Her eyes softened, the love he'd seen on oh so many days and nights reflected in their depths. "I know you are angry with me, Mathias. Please understand, as much as I longed to, I couldn't leave you a note telling you how much I love you. How I want to be your wife and accept your marriage proposal—until I was able to convince the King that he should reward you with me. It is something my father often does—gives his daughters away in marriage as gifts or rewards. And I do love you, Mathias. So very much. I swear that from now on, there will be no more secrets between us."

Mischief twinkled in her dark eyes. "You know, I've been told I should be honest with my future husband. That I shouldn't try to trick him on our wedding night. I think it's only right that I inform you, I'm not a virgin."

His lips twitched as he fought back a smile. "We have something in common. Neither am I."

"I also want you to know I have a difficult time sleeping at night. Especially if there is something hard in my bed."

Mathias couldn't hold back his smile. "That's understandable. I've heard that beautiful princesses are very sensitive that way. I fear I may exacerbate the problem, Princess."

"Princess of snow?" she gently teased.

"Princess of my heart. Princess that I love. The only Princess for me."

"And will you ride off with her, taking her from this palace, and bring her to your castle?"

"Indeed." He took her hand and placed it over his heart. "I will bring her to my kingdom, the one we create with our very own magic, where I shall cherish and love her—ever after."

A promise Mathias sealed with a searing kiss.

HISTORICAL TIDBIT

Believe it or not, the ban on the game of Basset was real. King Louis XIV had a problem on his hands. Gaming tables had become very popular during his reign. Too many noble families were being ruined. In 1691, Louis XIV banned the game. I've taken artistic license in this story and moved the ban a few years earlier to 1687.

The character of Renault de Sard in this story (and in *The Marquis's New Clothes*) is based entirely on the first Lieutenant General of Police of Paris, Gabriel Nicolas de la Reynie. The office was inaugurated in 1667. Long before London's Bow Street Runners (formed in 1749), seventeenth century Paris had a police force whose job it was to protect the public. Good thing. Murders happened in Paris daily. Reynie's advanced views of law enforcement helped establish the foundation of modern policing.

So, why have I set the Fiery Tales series during the reign of King Louis XIV of France? Well, the glittering court of Louis XIV wasn't just salacious and elegant. This was the very time period that the father of fairy tales, Charles Perrault—author of *The Tales of Mother Goose*—wrote stories that have delighted generations: *Sleeping Beauty, Little Red Riding Hood, Puss in Boots,*

Bluebeard and the ever popular *Cinderella*, to name a few.

I hope you enjoyed your time in the opulent world when fairy tales were born. Please see the end for a delicious excerpt of yet another Fiery Tale!

Happy reading!

GLOSSARY

Antechamber   The sitting room in a lord's or lady's private apartments (chambers).

Basset   A card game banned by the King and played by the wealthy. It brought about the ruin of many people of quality.

Caleçons   Drawers/underwear.

Chambers   Another word for private apartments. A lord or lady's chambers consisted of a bedroom, a sitting room, a bathroom, and a cabinet (office) Some chambers were bigger and more elaborate than others. Some cabinets were so large, they were used for private meetings.

Chère   Dear one. A term of endearment for a woman (*cher* for a man).

Chérie   Darling or cherished one. A term of endearment for a woman (*chéri* for a man).

Couch   A term in the card game Basset. It's the first bet placed on any given card. Once a player wins his or her *couch*, they can either accept payment or let their money lie and go for a greater stakes, like a *sept-et-le-va*—seven times the original bet.

Dieu   God.

Justacorps   A man's fitted knee-length coat, worn over his vest and breeches.

Hôtel/Château   A mansion located in the city. Members of the upper class and the wealthy bourgeois (middle class) often had a hôtel in Paris in addition to a palatial country estate (*château*).

Lettre de Cachet Orders/letters of confinement—without trial—signed by the King with the royal seal (*cachet*).

Ma belle   My beauty. Endearment for a woman.

Merde   Shit.

Salle   Room.

Salle de Bain   Bathroom. A small room located in one's private apartments in either a château or hôtel. The room usually had a fireplace, a tub, and a toilet (that looked like a chair with a chamber pot). The room was small on purpose so that the fire from the fireplace would keep the space warm while one bathed.

READ AN EXCERPT OF
THREE RECKLESS WISHES

Inspired by Charles Perrault's classic fairy tale, *"Three Wishes"*, a erotically charged historical romance in the acclaimed Fiery Tales Series...A scorching tale of redemption and undeniable desire...

Luc de Moutier, Marquis of Fontenay, is haunted by the writings of a dead woman. He is the subject of her romantic interest. Obsessed with her journal, he can't stop thinking about the sweetly sensual words of the late Isabelle Laurent. Though he'd never noticed her watching him from afar, he now compares every woman to the innocent enchantress who invades his thoughts and most luscious dreams . . .

A Guarded Secret...

The old Isabelle is dead. Sought after by the most powerful men in the realm, Isabelle has her choice of wealthy lovers. Her only goals are to provide for her young son, and to maintain the ruse of her demise. Three reckless wishes led her down the path she now walks. And there is no turning back. She allows her heart's yearnings to show only on the pages of her anonymously published books. Charming and witty, she dons her social mask each day, her performance unshakable until the very man of her long-held private dreams walks into her life—and shakes the foundations of her carefully crafted world.

An Unexpected Ecstasy…

When Luc meets the beautiful courtesan, she captures his fascination. He's determined to know the woman behind the facade. To deliciously decimate her defenses, show her his true passion and the depths of his desire—one exquisite carnal encounter at a time…But soon he discovers books written in a style all too familiar to him . . . and a passion as perilous as it is perfect.

CHAPTER ONE

Paris, 1661

... There are times I have dreamed of it. I am naked in his embrace. His hand moves down my body, warm fingers grazing lightly across my skin. The sensation is so sublime, I cannot contain my sound of bliss. I arch to him, hungry for more.

He alone ignites this fire inside me, one I cannot extinguish. Anymore than I can stop these vivid dreams—so shamelessly unbridled. Nor can I quash the feelings he stirs within my heart.

Oh, how I long for his heart, his smile. His arms around me. I want to know the feel of his skin, the taste of his kiss.

I want to indulge in all the carnal delights he favors.

I want to surrender to his every wicked desire.

Down to my very marrow, I feel there is a connection between us. One destined in the stars. If he would simply notice me, touch me, he would feel it, too ...

Marc d'Emery, Marquis de Vigneau, slammed the journal shut. "*Merde.* I can't read anymore, Luc. I'm at a full cockstand and we're just minutes from my sister's hôtel." He tossed the journal across the moving carriage to the empty spot next to Luc de Moutier, Marquis de Fontenay. "I'll admit it. That's stirring stuff—and I can understand the appeal of her writing—but the last woman you should be thinking about is a dead one."

Luc tightened his jaw as he stared out the window. A blur of gray townhomes and indistinguishable people threaded past as dusk descended. He agreed. He should have ceased his fascination with the journal, and more importantly, with the author of the evocative writing long ago.

In the almost two years since Sabine, his brother's new wife, had given Luc the journal, he'd read it so many times, he had the blasted thing memorized. He couldn't seem to put it away and forget about it. Forget about *her*.

Isabelle Laurent.

Sabine's deceased twin.

He was the subject of Isabelle's writings. The object of her desire, and affection. It completely staggered him that these passionate posts had been written by a female completely untried and unschooled in the carnal arts. And just as astonishing was the affinity she'd had for him.

One he'd known absolutely nothing about.

He hadn't even known Isabelle existed until Sabine had entered his brother Jules's life and Luc learned all about his sister-in-law's only sibling. *Jésus-Christ*, the late famous playwright, Paul Laurent, had been Sabine's and Isabelle's father. Luc had attended Paul Laurent's theater more times than he could count. He hadn't even been aware that the man had daughters at all—despite having spoken to him countless times.

And not once—not one bloody time—while Isabelle had watched him from the side of the stage with such adoration and tender desire, recording every little tidbit she observed about him, had he noticed her.

Not a single sighting. Not even a glimpse.

All the while she'd duly noted what he wore. Which of her father's plays he appeared to like. Which parts made him laugh.

Deriving such astute deductions about his personal tastes.

Deriving such astute deductions about far more—things the rest of the world didn't see about him.

The more he'd learned about her from her journal, the more he wanted to know her and was amazed how akin her own personal tastes were to his. On so many subjects.

For a woman he'd never met, he knew her better than any female who had ever entered his life. For a woman who'd never once spoken to him, she knew him better than anyone else ever had.

How absurd is that?

She came to life on the pages of her journal. And he couldn't help but wonder, more times than he could count, about the sound of her voice, or her laugh. The feel of *her* skin.

Her taste.

All the things he'd never know about her were tormenting him.

Isabelle Laurent and her enthralling journal, documenting the last year of Isabelle's life, had him completely beguiled.

And utterly burning.

Just having the thing near him tightened his groin and warmed his blood. He didn't have to look down at the brown leather-bound volume on the seat next to him to know it was there. He sensed it. Was all too aware of it. And *her*. She was in his thoughts constantly.

It was completely illogical, but he actually *mourned* the loss of her. The loss of ever getting to know her.

Worst of all, his fascination with Isabelle Laurent hadn't diminished over time. It had only strengthened. He wanted a dead woman.

Dieu, he had no bloody idea how to alter this lamentable state. How the hell did he get her out of his system?

He had a vague description of her: dark hair and eyes—a sharp contrast to her twin sister's fair coloring. In his mind's eye he'd formed a mental image of Isabelle Laurent—and that very same dark-haired, dark-eyed beauty was making appearances in every one of his erotic dreams. Passages from her journal playing out in the most vivid, mind-melting detail.

Each time he'd wake up alone, his cock stiff as a spike, the pressure in his sac immense. Ravenous for her.

For a woman he couldn't ever have.

One who'd been dead for six years and who was haunting him in the most maddening ways.

If he'd caught her watching him—just once—he might not be so tormented with what ifs. If she hadn't perished at the hands of a madman who was now thankfully dead and gone, she'd still be here.

Leon de Vittry had left so much devastation in his wake. A sickening number of innocent women he'd murdered had been discovered at the bottom of his privy, the natural smells having masked the stench of death. He may have spared Isabelle that particular indignity when he murdered her. But her fiery death at the hands of that fucking monster had been no less horrific.

It had taken five long years to learn that de Vittry had murdered Isabelle. And to prove de Vittry had had a hand in the conspiracy against Luc's family that ultimately led not only to the false treason charges laid against his father Charles de Moutier.

But to his execution as a traitor to the Crown, as well.

The irony was committing treason had been about the only sin not on Luc's father's lengthy list of transgressions.

The *only* accusation he hadn't deserved.

And he didn't shed a single tear over his father's death—or rather *the devil*—as he'd often called him in the quiet of his mind since boyhood. He hated his piece of *merde* father. Charles de Moutier had caused more than his own share of human suffering and deserved punishment he got. There was no doubt in Luc's mind that at this very moment he was standing right next to de Vittry—burning in hell.

After all he'd been through with his father and family's disgrace, his life had *finally* been set right. He and Jules had regained favor with the King. Reclaimed their family's vast fortune that had been confiscated. And cleared their sullied name as enemies of the Crown. During their miserable exile from Paris, when polite society had turned its back on them, when he and Jules had been stripped of everything including their dignity, nobility—and for a time their freedom during their own arrests—Luc had not only longed to reform the Moutiers' ruined reputation, but to take it to new heights of power and prestige.

To that end, he knew he should find a wife with exalted bloodlines and vast wealth. A union that would enhance his family's esteem and already laden coffers.

The problem was, he just couldn't stop comparing each suitable choice to Isabelle—when it shouldn't matter that the women didn't have the same wit, intellect and natural sensuality as the deceased dark-haired beauty dominating his mind day and night.

"Are you absolutely certain you never saw Isabelle at Laurent's theater?" Mentally, Luc cringed. The question had fallen out of his mouth, uncensored. *Damn it. Just let this go.* His words sounded pathetic even in his own ears. It was laced with desperation. A desperation to learn more—*anything more*—about the elusive and far too captivating Isabelle Laurent.

He'd spent his entire life maintaining a certain level of detachment—from everyone. He liked women. The women who'd graced his life had been his greatest source of joy. He loved discovering all the interesting little quirks and habits that made each one unique. And then there were those delicious sweet spots on their body, the ones that made them moan for him.

He adored discovering those even more.

He never deceived women. Never made promises he would not keep, and always made it clear that his interest was in a carnal connection—unbridled mutual pleasure.

Without emotional entanglement.

He was most at ease when he controlled his world. Soft feelings made him shirk away. A long time ago, he'd learned to keep a tight rein on his emotions at all times.

Or else...

What Isabelle had done to him, the tender feelings her writings had inspired, was beyond unsettling. And he was too damned seasoned to be this unraveled by the mere words of an ingénue.

Smiling good-naturedly, Marc shook his head, the shade of his dark, curly hair likely to have been very similar to Isabelle's own locks. "Luc, I'm beginning to worry about you. This obsession you have with this dead woman isn't at all healthy. Why don't you focus on, say...*a live one*? They're much easier to bed."

Luc sighed, frustrated. "I know it's been years since the theater closed and the playwright passed away, but surely *someone* caught a glimpse of her? A young dark-haired woman who perhaps resembled Laurent a little?" He had no idea if she'd resembled her father at all. Paul Laurent's prestigious theater had been highly popular among the upper class before the civil unrest—the *Fronde*—when all of Paris went mad. And Luc's world collapsed around him.

Marc shrugged. "And what if they did? What difference does it make?"

He wished he knew the answer to that. He had no idea why learning more about this deceased young woman should matter at all.

Marc leaned in and rested his elbows on his thighs, his smile returning. "You know what you need?

To stop thinking about Isabelle Laurent . . . "What?"

"To commence negotiations with the Duc d'Allain for a marriage contract between you and his daughter Sophie—"

Luc groaned. "Good Lord. No, not her. Unless she has changed since my exile, the woman speaks incessantly. There's only so much inane conversation a man can tolerate about her shoes."

Marc chuckled. "Aside from her somewhat wanting conversational skills, she is a beauty. Claiming your conjugal rights won't be much of a hardship." He grinned.

"Unless she's still taking about her footwear while I'm fucking her."

That garnered a bark of laughter from his friend. "All right. Forget the Duc d'Allain's daughter," Marc said, still softly chuckling. "What you need, my friend, is to enjoy yourself tonight. This masque is a perfect place for you to reenter society. You can mingle about with anonymity, reacquaint yourself with old friends, and perhaps make some new ones."

He didn't have any old friends.

The few Luc had once trusted turned their backs, distancing themselves from him as soon as they'd arrested Charles for treason. Though the King's pardon had come almost two years ago, Luc had stayed away from Paris. Spending every moment seeing to the extensive restorations his properties desperately needed after years of abandonment and neglect while in the Crown's possession.

He'd refused to reenter society until everything was perfect.

He had to show them that despite his banishment from Paris, and his imprisonment before that, he had not broken. He'd not only restored his chateaus, he'd brought them beyond their former glory.

Better still, he'd destroyed and removed anything that reminded him of Charles from his childhood homes.

"What new friends are there to make?" he asked. No doubt there would be some who'd still be leery of socializing with a man whose family had been labeled traitors to king and country.

His former short temper with the male aristocracy, and his quickness to duel, had never made him overly popular among the men in his class.

His popularity had come from the finer sex. With whom he's always felt the most at ease.

"Well, Juliette Carre comes to mind. She is one woman you *need* to meet."

Luc crossed his arms casually. "Oh? Why do I *need* to meet Juliette Carre?"

"Because she doesn't talk incessantly about footwear. In fact, she has everyone in Paris completely charmed. And she's a courtesan," Marc added.

Luc lifted a brow. Marc was well aware he'd sworn off his old ways. His days as an unrepentant libertine, bedding beauties around the realm, were over. He wanted nothing to detract him from his plans. Or the new image he wanted to forge.

Merde. He was distracted enough by Isabelle Laurent and her bewitching journal.

"Now wait." Marc held up his hand. "I know your 'plan' and what you're thinking. Allow me to explain the benefit here. Though there are plenty of courtesans around, this one is different. In truth, rather exceptional—a vision, with a polished wit to match. Luc, you've got to see her. When she enters the room, she is utterly enthralling. Every man of consequence is vying for her. And she is very selective. Any man who beds her has the immediate respect and regard of every male in the realm. A definite boon for you should she favor you. I heard that the Duc de Savard gave her a significant sum—without ever bedding her—just to be considered as her next choice. And two weeks ago, the Marquis de Renier and the Comte de Northy practically came to a duel over the Comte's refusal to relinquish his seat beside her to the Marquis, despite being outranked socially. After everything that's happened, if you really want to make a grand impression, bed Juliette Carre." Marc's usual smile returned. "She's one woman who won't bore you. She'll be here tonight. If there's anyone who can make you forget all about Isabelle Laurent, the beautiful and captivating Juliette most certainly can."

Dieu. He'd be willing to pay a King's ransom to snap the spell Isabelle's journal had cast on him. How he wished simply bedding a courtesan would do that. Luc glanced down at the brown leather-bound item resting beside him on the velvet seat. Looking so deceptively innocuous.

It had the most powerful pull on him.

It was so potent, no one, not even the newest most coveted courtesan in Paris, no matter how charming or beautiful, would be able to obliterate it.

THANK YOU for reading THE PRINCESS AND THE DIAMONDS!

Want my next release for just **99¢?** Sign up for my **99¢ New Release Alert** newsletter at www.LilaDiPasqua.com. Each new release will be **99¢** for a SHORT time only. Get notified. Don't miss out!

FIERY TALES SERIES

Novellas
Sleeping Beau
Little Red Writing
Bewitching in Boots
The Marquis's New Clothes
The Lovely Duckling
The Princess and the Diamonds

Holiday Novella
The Duke's Match Girl

Anthologies
Awakened by a Kiss
The Princess in His Bed

Full-length novels
A Midnight Dance
Undone
Three Reckless Wishes

Lila DiPasqua is a *USA TODAY* bestselling author of historical romance with heat. She lives with her husband, three children and two rescued dogs and is a firm believer in the happily-ever-after. You can find her on Facebook, Twitter, Instagram, and Goodreads!